CW00815966

WINNING SKYHUNTER

Stonefire Dragons Universe #1

by Jessie Donovan

This book is a work of fiction. Names, characters, places, and incidents are either the product of the writer's imagination or are used fictitiously, and any resemblance to actual persons, living or dead, business establishments, events, or locales is entirely coincidental.

Winning Skyhunter

Mythical Lake Press, LLC
First Digital Edition

Cover Art by Clarissa Yeo of Yocla Designs
ISBN: 978-1942211754

Books by Jessie Donovan

Love in Scotland

Crazy Scottish Love (LiS #1)
Chaotic Scottish Wedding (LiS #2)

Asylums for Magical Threats

Blaze of Secrets (AMT #1)
Frozen Desires (AMT #2)
Shadow of Temptation (AMT #3)
Flare of Promise (AMT #4)

Cascade Shifters

Convincing the Cougar (CS #0.5)
Reclaiming the Wolf (CS #1)
Cougar's First Christmas (CS #2)
Resisting the Cougar (CS #3)

Kelderan Runic Warriors

The Conquest (KRW #1)
The Barren (KRW #2)
The Heir (KRW #3)
The Forbidden (KRW #4)
The Hidden / Vala & Thorin (KRW #5 / 2019)

Lochguard Highland Dragons

The Dragon's Dilemma (LHD #1)
The Dragon Guardian (LHD #2)
The Dragon's Heart (LHD #3)
The Dragon Warrior (LHD #4)

The Dragon Family (LHD #5)
The Dragon's Discovery / Alistair Boyd (LHD #6 / 2019)

Stonefire Dragons

Sacrificed to the Dragon (SD #1)
Seducing the Dragon (SD #2)
Revealing the Dragons (SD #3)
Healed by the Dragon (SD #4)
Reawakening the Dragon (SD #5)
Loved by the Dragon (SD #6)
Surrendering to the Dragon (SD #7)
Cured by the Dragon (SD #8)
Aiding the Dragon (SD #9)
Finding the Dragon (SD #10)
Craved by the Dragon (SD #11)
Persuading the Dragon / Zain & Ivy (SD #12 / 2020)

CHAPTER ONE

Asher King stood about twenty feet away from a two-story rectangular, brick building and clenched his fingers into fists. At one time, he'd vowed to never set foot inside the main security building for Clan Skyhunter ever again. And yet, here he was, about to go willingly.

His gaze drifted to the barely aboveground window, reinforced with steel bars. The corridor and set of rooms behind it were more than familiar to him. After all, he'd been chained inside a cell for more than five years, constantly drugged to prevent his inner dragon from doing more than stumbling about inside his head, never being able to shift.

All because he'd disagreed with the clan leader and how he treated the clan.

His inner dragon stirred and spoke inside his mind. *We have a chance to fix his mistakes and make things better.*

Are you sure? Because entering our former prison is only the first step of a very long, difficult road.

His beast huffed. *Of course I'm sure. Otherwise, who knows what will happen to the clan? They need a good leader if we're to rebuild. We would do a good job.*

Asher had agonized for weeks, debating if he would be able to overcome his past and have a chance at winning the leadership position of Clan Skyhunter. His own physical strength, as well as his dragon's stamina, weren't the only obstacles. No, the former clan leader Marcus King was his uncle.

No matter that Asher had stood up to the bastard and tried to reach out to the Department of Dragon Affairs for help, many of those still living on Skyhunter saw only his name.

Blood will tell, some said. *Marcus was once a good leader, too.*

His dragon growled. *Just stop. We would never allow a human to bury dead bodies on our land, let alone jail and abuse any clan member.*

All things Marcus had done, all for his own personal gain. *I know that. However, at the first sign of strain or anything being too much for us to handle, you tell me straightaway.*

I'm strong enough. I always will be.

Dragon…

His beast paused. At one time, Asher would've known exactly how his inner dragon would act. But after five years of being separated because of drugs, they were still testing each other out and determining how they fit together again.

Almost every other contender for the leadership position didn't have the same handicap.

It was the single biggest reservation Asher had about trying to win the right to be clan leader. After all, Asher didn't smile as often or joke around like he had before the imprisonment. Who knew what the long-term drugs had done to his dragon's mind.

His beast huffed. *We may not be exactly the same, but I'm still honorable. I would never endanger others merely to boost my ego. I would rather die first.*

His dragon's reassurance eased his nerves a little. *And that's all I need to hear.*

Right, then let's go. We can't be late, or we'll never have a chance. The smallest mistake or mishap will disqualify us from the trials.

Adjusting the ridiculous tie around his neck—it and the suit he wore were a requirement put forth by the deciding council—Asher headed straight for the main entrance to the Protectors' security building.

He nearly paused at the doorway as images of his dark, dirty prison cell, shared with several other males, filled his mind. Males who had sometimes broken down sobbing after a torture session. Others who had started to show signs of madness because of the silence of their dragons. And then those who had lost all hope, simply giving up on life itself.

Asher had come close, so close to lashing out toward the end. He might not have survived whole if Marcus had been in charge of the clan too much longer.

His beast spoke up. *But he's gone, which is all that matters. You didn't break. You're strong.* His beast stood taller inside his mind. *I'm glad you're my human.*

At the love and pride emanating from his inner beast, Asher smiled. *And I'm happy you're my dragon. Well, most of the time.*

Before his beast could protest, Asher crossed the threshold and walked quickly to the main conference room. It was where all the clan leader candidates would meet with their liaison from the Department of Dragon Affairs, which was the branch of the UK government that dealt with and handled the dragon-shifters.

The DDA didn't usually concern themselves with clan leader trials. Most of their efforts were spent with the human sacrifice programs, where human females willingly allowed a dragonman to impregnate them in exchange for a vial of valuable dragon's blood that could heal many human illnesses.

In recent months, from what Asher had been able to gather since being set free, the DDA had spent just as much effort on finding and subduing those out to destroy or enslave dragon-shifters as they did on their other priorities. The news reports stated how short-staffed they were most of the time, too.

However, even with those tasks taking up much of their time, the previous corruption of both the Skyhunter leader and the former DDA Director warranted extraordinary caution. No one wanted a repeat performance.

Hence the DDA's oversight regarding the Skyhunter trials.

His beast huffed. *How long will it take for others to stop blaming us all for Marcus's treachery?*

I don't know. But getting angry won't do anything. Channel the energy into the trials.

Asher reached the entrance to the large conference room and nodded to the male standing guard. Robin had been a prisoner under Marcus's reign like Asher, although they hadn't been cellmates.

They shared a look of understanding. Regardless of who became leader, no clan member would ever be imprisoned again for simply expressing an opinion.

Once inside the room, Asher did a quick scan. There were seven other candidates: five males and two females. While he knew all of them, it was the blonde-haired, blue-eyed female at the end of the table who caught his eye.

She may be older and now an adult, but he'd recognize Honoria Wakeham anywhere.

Although where she'd come from, he didn't know. Her parents had sent her to America nearly fifteen years ago for her safety, back when she'd been a teenager and Marcus had only started to make questionable decisions.

Honoria's gaze met his, the widening of her eyes telling him she knew who he was, too.

His dragon spoke up. *I want to talk to her.*

Not now.

Soon? I've missed her. And she's even prettier than before. Very pretty. Maybe you can finally end your dry spell with her.

It's not really a dry spell when you're imprisoned for five years, he drawled.

Of course, Asher wasn't sure he could mentally handle a female just yet, regardless. No one wanted to wake up next to a male screaming from his nightmares.

Pushing aside thoughts of nightmares and sex, Asher quickly took the remaining empty chair on one side of the table, next to one of the males.

As soon as he took his seat, a young woman who couldn't be more than twenty-five stood and cleared her throat. All he knew was that she was one of the human DDA employees. "Good afternoon. My name is Penny, and thank you all for coming, especially since I know this isn't the usual method of how you select a clan leader. However, I think we can all agree that whoever becomes clan leader of Skyhunter must be willing to work with the DDA, as well as the other clans in the UK, to prevent another scandal. In fact, as we progress, the other UK clan leaders will make appearances and talk with you. They will help in the final decision-making process, although it will ultimately be up to the DDA to determine who is allowed to take command."

All the dragon-shifters sat in silence. The DDA employee's undertone was understood. This was the last chance for Skyhunter to redeem themselves. While it had been centuries since the last occurrence, dragon-shifter clans had been disbanded in the past, and theirs could very well be the next one.

Asher's beast spoke up. *We will* not *fail. Everyone who remains on Skyhunter is anxious to rebuild and move forward.*

I'm not sure if everyone is the right word, but enough of them.

The DDA had already removed all of the co-conspirators several months ago. Thankfully, it had been a much smaller number than Asher had first imagined.

Penny spoke up again, looking at each candidate in turn. "Today will be the interview portion of the trials. The first candidate, Lee, will come with me now."

Lee stood. Without a backward glance, he left with the DDA employee, leaving the remaining candidates in the room.

At first, silence descended and stayed that way. However, Asher glanced down at the other end of the table, meeting Honoria's gaze. Having learned not to waste what life he had remaining, he asked, "So when did you get back, Ria?"

Honoria Wakeham was a stranger in her own clan.

Her parents had detected Marcus's changing behavior fifteen years ago and had sent Honoria to live with distant cousins in America. While she'd never quite felt at home with Clan WildCanyon near San Francisco, she'd done her best to make a new life in California. Yes, her accent had always set her apart, as had her name—no American was ever called Honoria in the modern age. But she'd made friends, earned a degree in business, and had been on the cusp of launching a joint venture between the American Department of Dragon Affairs for the West Coast region and Clan WildCanyon. She'd just about set her life in motion, toward a more permanent standing with the American dragon-shifters, when news of Clan Skyhunter's upheaval and Marcus King's removal had reached the States.

As soon as she'd heard of the upcoming clan leader trials, Honoria's gut and dragon had urged her to return home. Still, she'd been on the fence. No female had led a dragon-shifter clan in recent memory.

However, with news of a female clan leader's existence—Teagan O'Shea—and her actions spreading around the world, that had been the final push she'd needed to pick up her life once again and return to England. Being female was no longer a reason to not lead a clan, especially as more and more of Teagan's deeds in Ireland became known.

Her dragon spoke up. *Of course females can lead. It's silly to think otherwise.*

You thinking we can lead and others accepting it are two different things. However, Teagan taking down the corrupt Irish clan leaders has proven to all that a female can be strong, too.

Her dragon sniffed and fell silent.

Honoria went back to rhythmic breathing to calm her nerves as she waited in the conference room for things to begin. And then the last person she'd thought to see take part in the trials walked in.

Asher King.

At one time they'd been friends. More than friends, to be honest. However, Honoria had been whisked away to a different country without being able to say goodbye to him.

As an adult, she understood her parents' caution and need to act quickly. But as a teenage girl in love, it had devastated her for nearly a year.

Her dragon murmured, *But he's here now.*

Right, and now he's a rival. Besides, I'm sure an honorable male like him would've found his mate by now.

Her beast's voice turned soft. *Not unless someone had been willing to wait five years for him be set free.*

Not long after Honoria had arrived back on Skyhunter, she'd heard details about the former leader's reign that hadn't made it to the international media—torture, imprisonment, and deliberately baiting some clan members against each other. It couldn't have been easy for any honorable dragon-shifter to survive.

However, before her thoughts strayed to all the rumors she'd heard, the DDA employee began talking.

It was only when the human had left that Honoria debated what to do. Talking with Asher—or any of the other candidates—would be a bad idea. She needed to remain impartial if she wanted any chance of winning the right to lead Skyhunter and bring them back from ruin.

Just as her dragon was about to speak, Asher's deep voice carried in the room. "So when did you get back, Ria?"

The syllables of how he said her nickname rolled over her. Unable to resist, she met his blue eyes.

As teenagers, they'd always been full of amusement or laughter. Now, she only saw hardness and determination.

She wondered exactly what horrors had happened to Asher under Marcus King's leadership. Something had turned the teasing, smiling boy into what he was now.

More than ever, she thought her parents had been right to send her away.

Too bad it wasn't the time or place to ask Asher for details. Instead, she kept her tone light as she replied, "I returned here a week ago."

He nodded. "Good to hear you still have your accent."

"I made a point to keep it. You'd be surprised how much Americans love to hear it."

Silence fell, and Honoria debated keeping the conversation going. She was curious to know more about her childhood boyfriend, and yet it would be better to keep her distance.

Her dragon spoke up. *I don't want to keep our distance. He's harder, more intense. I want him.*

Since Honoria didn't sense any urgency or constant need from her beast, she had a feeling Asher wasn't her true mate.

Usually a kiss let a dragon-shifter know if a person was their true mate. If so, it would kick off a mate-claim frenzy, which was more like a sex marathon until the female was finally pregnant.

Yes, she'd kissed Asher as a young girl, but frenzies only happened after a female hit twenty years of age or so.

Her dragon chimed in. *I don't want a true mate. There's too much to do if we win the clan leadership, and a mate would only distract us.*

I agree completely.

But that doesn't mean I don't want to kiss him again. Imagine all that intensity. It would be delicious.

Asher's voice interrupted her conversation with her dragon. "Why come back now? Last I heard, you were a rising star back in California."

Her dragon stood tall. *He kept track of us.*

Hush.

She glanced at the others in the room, but none of them met her eyes. "If you're looking for a weakness to exploit, I'm not going to give it, Ash."

His lips curled in a bittersweet smile. "Few people call me Ash anymore."

One of the male candidates muttered, "Because you're a King, and need to be reminded of it."

Honoria should keep her mouth shut. After all, defending Asher could bring trouble later on. However, the words spilled from her lips before she could stop it. "As if your family is free of treason, Shane. Your older brother was head Protector under Marcus, after all."

Shane Farhall turned his head toward Honoria, hatred in his eyes. "Which is why I'm here, to right things. However, King's family gave the orders. My brother either had to follow them or be imprisoned himself."

Asher's tone was almost bored when he jumped in. "Your brother could've spoken up, like I did." Bitterness filled his next words. "But no, he didn't. Instead, he helped bury dead bodies on our land. Human bodies, no less. He had control of all the security forces on Skyhunter, but didn't do anything to actually protect the clan."

Shane stood, turning toward Asher. "Everyone knows about your uncle being clan leader, but what about your cousin?" He leaned forward and snarled, "While never formally declared, everyone knows he tortured the prisoners."

"I know. I was one of the prisoners, remember? Blood doesn't always equal family, especially under tyranny," Asher stated.

"You could say that and no one would be the wiser. I'm sure you received special treatment, unlike the dozen males who died during their imprisonment."

Asher's pupils flashed to slits and back. "Special treatment? Try being kept in a bright, white room for days on end, music grating and never ceasing. It pushes your dragon to the brink. Not that you'd know it, Shane. You were busy hiding in Wales."

Honoria's dragon spoke up. *If we don't do something, they may end up killing each other.*

Normally, Honoria would call out her dragon's hyperbole. However, Shane's temper had been infamous even as a child. She didn't doubt he'd risk him and his dragon to get revenge for his brother's life sentence inside a DDA prison. In Shane's mind, killing one member of the King family would make them even.

Her dragon huffed. *That sort of thinking belongs to the dragon-shifters of old, not in the twenty-first century.*

Reason has nothing to do with it, dragon. Male emotions and revenge have started many a war in the past.

Before she could think of how to intervene, Asher crossed his arms and looked straight ahead of him at the wall. "Save your strength for the trials. If you truly believe you're better than me, then prove it."

She resisted blinking. The older version of Asher was mostly...level-headed. Wise, even.

Her beast purred, *I like it. He was okay to kiss as a teenager, but I'm more interested in the grown male.*

Studying Asher's profile, she noticed a smattering of scars near his jaw. *I wonder if that's from when he was a prisoner.*

If so, he's not going to tell us. Males are stubborn.

Right, because female dragons are never *stubborn, are they?* Honoria drawled.

Her beast sniffed. *All dragons are stubborn to some extent. However, males are stubborn for the sake of it. Almost as if they think it makes them more macho or something.*

Honoria didn't think Asher would be stubborn for the sake of it. *If his scars are a result of torture, then of course he doesn't want to talk about it.*

And it hit her—Asher had spent at least five years as a prisoner. True, she'd heard about it. But as she stared at his profile, making out the pattern of scars on his jaw, it became more than words. Those faint white marks were only a fraction of the proof of what he'd endured.

Proof that the male sitting not far from her wasn't the teenage boy she'd snuck out to kiss when she could.

Her dragon's voice was soft when she said, *That's not a bad thing. He is a survivor.*

Yes, but I'm also concerned about his mental health. I want to believe Asher is a good candidate, but it's only been six months since Marcus was deposed and the prisoners were released.

All the more reason to seek him out later and talk.

I'm sure talking is all you're thinking about.

I wouldn't mind some release. It's been too long.

I'm not going to feel guilty about that. I had to get everything squared away back in America before coming home to England.

Her dragon grunted and curled up into a ball inside her mind, closing her eyes to feign sleep.

The DDA human, Penny, returned alone and called out Asher's name. Honoria watched him walk out the door for his one-on-one interview. While his stride was confident, she wondered what it could be masking deep inside.

Maybe once she was done with her interview, she would seek him out. After all, one of the marks of a good clan leader was talking with clan members and judging how things were going.

So talking with Asher would merely be practice, in case she won. Yes, just practice. It had nothing to do with her own curiosity.

Her dragon snorted. *Liar.*

Ignoring her beast, Honoria sat quietly and practiced her breathing techniques once more. Doing well in the interview was more important than anything. And to do her best, she needed to purge her mind of Asher King and the scars on his jaw.

CHAPTER TWO

As Asher walked into one of the Protector offices being used by the DDA for the day, it took every iota of strength he possessed not to think of another interview conducted in the same building. The one nearly six years ago which had sealed his fate, when he hadn't denied wanting to overthrow Marcus King.

His dragon growled. *This will determine our future, and one of our choosing. Don't fuck it up.*

I don't plan to. Now, shut it. I need to concentrate.

Sitting down in the chair across from Penny, Asher waited patiently for what happened next.

The human female cleared her throat and looked at the paper on her clipboard. A second later, she met his gaze. "So, Mr. Asher King, tell me why you want to be the leader of Clan Skyhunter."

On the surface, the question was easy. However, the way a person answered could reveal a lot about one's character. Torture at the hand of his bastard cousin had at least taught him that.

He replied, "I want to make Skyhunter respectable and trusted again, like it was when I was a young child. I've done my best over the last few months to catch up with everything that happened during my imprisonment, and

I'm confident the future lies with working with the other British dragon-shifter clans."

Penny cleared her throat again. "Ah, yes. Your imprisonment. To be honest, that concerns everyone at the DDA. No matter how honorable your intentions, they will mean nothing if you suddenly become unstable as a result of your, ah, your..."

Her voice trailed off, so Asher finished the sentence. "Torture."

The human female shifted in her seat. She was clearly uncomfortable about the topic.

However, tiptoeing around the issue wouldn't help his case. Asher spoke again. "I've been seeing the counselor here on loan from Clan Snowridge." Snowridge was the dragon clan in the North of Wales. "You can speak with Dr. Allonby about my sessions, if you wish. However, I have control of both my mind and my dragon. I wouldn't have put my name in the running if I didn't."

The human shuffled through a stack of papers. He wished they would've sent someone with more experience, or at the very least a human with the confidence needed to oversee the trials. Those vying for clan leader wouldn't be meek, silent, biddable individuals.

Of course, most humans acted strangely around a dragon-shifter. It was ridiculous, really, since it wasn't as if he was going to suddenly shift and make her his supper.

His beast grunted. *Dragons haven't eaten humans for over ten thousand years.*

Shush.

Penny must not have noticed his flashing dragon eyes and carried on as normal. "I will check in with the counselor later. Now, let me test your knowledge of both DDA policy and the laws concerning dragon-shifters in the United Kingdom."

As the human asked one question after another, Asher answered them without thinking. He'd always had the knack of memorizing something once he'd read it. The skill had helped stave off boredom and madness during his imprisonment since he could remember a book almost word-for-word and replay it inside his head.

All too soon the female was finished and dismissed him. The interview seemed rather pointless, truth be told. And if any of the candidates couldn't pass this phase, which wasn't more than a memory test, they were weak indeed.

His dragon spoke up. *The DDA must be thorough. It's a human thing.*

Any fool can memorize the rules, but you're right. Maybe Shane will fail the first test and we won't have to worry about him.

You shouldn't let him get to you.

Asher finally exited the central security building and walked purposefully toward the main living area of the clan. *He ran away whereas we stayed and tried to do our best to fight Marcus.*

True, but it's easier to blame someone else for something going wrong than to admit their own role in it.

He snorted. *When did you become so wise?*

I couldn't talk whilst under the drugs, but I could think. After all those years, I could be a bloody philosophy professor by now.

Oh, no. I don't think so. I want to be useful, and pondering the meaning of life or the universe isn't going to change anything here.

His beast grunted and turned his back. Asher should've reached out and soothed his beast, but they'd reached his mother's house, and the last thing he wanted to do was have his dragon eyes flashing while visiting his sister.

Doing his best to keep the sadness from his face, he entered and headed toward the kitchen. Sure enough, his mother was baking and chatting to a silent figure sitting at the dining table.

His mum noticed him and smiled. "Asher, how did it go?"

"Okay, I suppose. The real tests will come later."

His mother bobbed her head. "Well, sit down and I'll bring your lunch. Aimee has been waiting to see you today."

Aimee was Asher's much-younger sister. He sat down across from the female with the same dark hair and blue eyes as him. He reached across and touched her arm, but Aimee continued to stare blankly ahead as if he wasn't there.

Unlike Asher, his sister hadn't survived imprisonment with her dragon intact. Even worse, his sister hadn't spoken a word since being released.

Seeing his twenty-three-year-old baby sister staring into nothingness made him want to run out of the house, find his uncle and cousin, and make them pay. Aimee had only been fucking eighteen when they'd tossed her into a prison cell and drugged her dragon into a stupor. Since dragons didn't fully mature until twenty, everyone assumed his sister's inner beast hadn't been strong enough to fight for five years and come out mostly unscathed.

His dragon shuffled inside his mind, wanting to talk. But if he did, Asher's pupils would turn into slits and anytime Aimee saw flashing dragon eyes, she screamed and ran into her bedroom.

As he did every time he saw his sister, Asher took a few seconds to cool his anger, force a smile, and speak in a regular voice, free of worry or other negative emotion. "Hey, Aims. It's good to see you out of your room today. Maybe if the weather cooperates, I can take you around the clan soon, too." His sister remained silent, staring just past his shoulder. Patting her arm, he added, "I know you'll like it, especially with the sky mostly blue today."

From the corner of his eye, he saw his mother close her eyes and take a deep breath. With his father dead and his sister damaged, his mum didn't have an easy time of it.

Which was all the more motivation to try his best to win the clan leadership. He needed to make things better for his family, not to mention all the other families torn asunder by Marcus's leadership.

Standing, he went to help his mum in the kitchen. He may be vying for the most powerful position in Skyhunter, but for the moment, helping his mother was more important.

Honoria finished her interview quickly and exited the clan's security building.

The questions in the interview had been almost too easy. Still, there were many phases left, and she wasn't about to let her guard down and make a stupid mistake.

However, as she stood on the main road to the living area, the one that branched off into three directions, she debated making a teeny one.

Asher had been staying at his mother's house and had no doubt returned there. She should leave him alone and go home. Her uncle—a former Protector, in the days before Marcus King had been leader—had been helping her train. She had hours of exercises waiting for her.

And yet, her curiosity burned to talk alone with Asher, to see how he'd changed over the years.

Before she could realize her idiotic mistake and talk herself out of it, Honoria's feet turned her down the left fork in the path, the one which led to the King house.

Her dragon spoke up. *Good. If you didn't go see him, then you'd just keep thinking about him. And that would make any training we do useless.*

I could focus if I had to.

Maybe, maybe not. I know I would pester you until we finally saw him again.

Honoria mentally sighed. *I'm not going to sleep with him, dragon. So give it up already.*

Her beast huffed. *Why not? It'd be a good way to better know our competition.*

Right, I'm sure that's the main reason, she said slowly.

It could be. Her dragon paused and added more softly, *Besides, it will help him connect with his dragon. I sense the relationship is a bit strained there. Sex would bring them together.*

She waved at someone walking by. Ignoring their double-take—few knew Honoria had returned—she replied, *How can you even know that? Dragons can't read minds.*

No, but I just know. Call it a dragon's intuition.

She reached the two-story stone cottage where the Kings lived. It was a little apart from the rest of the houses in the area. Since Asher had lived in the more central part of the clan back in the day, his family must've moved to it sometime after she'd left.

For a second, she wondered if it was to isolate themselves a little from the accusations and looks of the clan. After all, Honoria didn't think Shane was the only dragon-shifter on Skyhunter to blame anyone with the King surname for what had happened.

Her beast spoke up. *Ask him if that's why they live here. It's that simple.*

Ignoring her dragon, she stopped at the door and knocked. A few beats later, the mostly gray-haired form of Lynne King, Asher's mother, filled the doorway. She instantly smiled at Honoria. “Ria, I had heard you were back, but it’s lovely to see you again.”

Memories of Lynne always welcoming her into their home flashed into Honoria’s mind. Asher’s mum was a link to the version of herself that had changed upon setting foot in America. “Hello, Mrs. King. I just came by to see if Asher was here?”

“He is.” She hesitated and glanced over her shoulder, and then back again. “But I’m not sure if my daughter can handle a visitor right now. Would you wait here a second? I’ll have Asher come to the door.”

As soon as she nodded, Lynne shut the door. The older female’s words made her wonder what had happened to Aimee, especially since no one had mentioned anything about Asher’s sister to her yet.

Before she could think too much on it, the door swung open. Asher frowned down at her. “What are you doing here?”

She raised an eyebrow. “Hello to you, too.”

He crossed his arms over his chest. A broad, muscled chest that tapered to a slim pair of hips. And she had no doubt beyond that were muscled thighs.

Asher King had matured well.

Her dragon hummed, but Honoria quickly constructed a temporary prison for her dragon, to prevent her beast from talking for a short while.

Asher grunted. “We’re rivals, Ria. You shouldn’t be here, and you know it.”

“Excuse me for wanting to stop by and say hello. You said a lot of cryptic stuff back in the conference room and I wanted some answers.”

“At least you’re not lying and trying to sweet talk me first.”

“When have I ever sweet-talked anyone?’

"I don't know, but you've been in America for over a decade. Who knows what you picked up."

It was on the tip of her tongue to say America was like anywhere, in that a clan was made up of all kinds of people. But arguing with Asher would accomplish nothing, nor was it important she win the point. "I merely wanted to say hello and ensure everything was okay, for old time's sake. I'm not here to execute any dirty tricks, I assure you."

Asher's mum appeared behind him. "Aimee went to her room for a nap, so won't you come in, Ria?"

"Mum, I don't think—"

She cut off her son. "I want to visit with her, even if you don't. And since you promised to help me with a few things in the kitchen, it means you'll have to tolerate her company, too."

Honoria studied Lynne. She hoped the female wasn't trying to matchmake. After all, it'd been more than fifteen years since she and Asher had dated.

Not to mention the small detail of them both vying for the clan leadership position.

Lynne gently pushed Asher aside and motioned in. "Come, Ria. I have some fresh biscuits that will go lovely with some proper tea. I can only imagine the horrid stuff you had to drink in America."

She smiled. "I do admit to missing the tea. My distant cousins didn't see the point in special ordering any, since everyone but me was a coffee drinker."

The older dragonwoman nodded. "Right, then that's settled. I'm going to give you as much tea as you can handle."

Lynne turned and walked down the hall. Asher didn't block the doorway but remained just to the side of it.

Honoria walked past him, a few scant inches between his body and hers. While it should be impossible, she felt the heat radiating from his body. Not to mention she picked up the spicy male scent that was purely Asher.

Their eyes locked and her heart skipped a beat. They were older and different, and yet her attraction to Asher hadn't changed. And judging by how his pupils flashed to slits and back, he was still drawn to her, too.

He was the first to break eye contact and take a step to the side, putting distance between them. Clearing her throat, Honoria went down the hall to what she could see was the kitchen.

It was a good thing her dragon was inside a mental prison currently, because she could only imagine her beast demanding to find somewhere private and ride Asher like there was no tomorrow.

And after the look she'd shared with him, she just might be tempted to do it without too much badgering from her dragon.

No. She couldn't allow attraction to derail her dreams or resolve. She may still be attracted to Asher, but she would restrain herself.

She had to. Otherwise, she'd never have the chance to help rebuild Skyhunter and make it greater than it ever had been before.

~~~

Asher watched Honoria's tall form walk down the hall, the sway of her hips making his beast roar inside his head.

She wants us as much as we do. We never had the chance to take her before. I think we should fuck her at least once.

His dragon was correct. As teenagers, they'd never crossed the line to full-on cock-in-pussy sex. And given the way Honoria had filled out in the hips and thighs, he wouldn't mind them wrapped around his waist.
~~~

Laughing, his beast spoke again. *I give you less than a week before you strip her naked and claim her.*

Warning bells went off inside his head. *She's not our true mate. Tell me she's not.*

No, I don't think so. But she'd be nice to claim all the same. She's as tall as us. It'll be nice to have all that female softness pressed up against us.

Stop, dragon. It's not going to happen. And not just because she's a rival.

So you do *want to fuck her. But if you're worried about the nightmares, they rarely come anymore.*

Rarely being the key word. No, I need to focus on healing myself before anything else.

She can help.

If you say her magical cunt will melt away all our troubles, I will toss you inside a mental cage in the next breath.

His dragon sniffed. *You wouldn't dare.*

I don't want to, but I will.

Since Asher only caged his beast as a last resort—he was trying to make up for the years they'd lost together—his dragon grunted in acknowledgment. *Fine. I won't tease you for the rest of the afternoon. However, don't be afraid. It's Ria, the female who knew us best.*

Knew is right. These days, neither of us are the same people.

His mother called out his name, and Asher strode toward the kitchen. Entering, he noticed Honoria sitting with her back to him. Her hair was pulled up in a ponytail, exposing the back of her neck. Once upon a time, she'd been ticklish there. He wondered if she still would be. All he had to do was close the distance between them and dance his fingers against her soft skin.

Brushing the thought aside, he went to stand next to his mother at the cooker. "Let me do this, Mum. Sit and chat with Ria."

"Join us, too, Asher, once the biscuits are ready."

"I will."

His mother gave him a skeptical look, but he did his best to look earnest. If the biscuits ended up taking an extraordinarily long time to cool, it would be an odd coincidence.

Coward, his dragon muttered.

His mother sat down and asked, "What have you been up too, Ria? I heard from your aunt how you were in charge of some fancy project back in the States."

From the corner of his eye, he watched the pair. Honoria shrugged. "I merely improved the communication systems between the American Department of Dragon Affairs and several clans on the west coast. I'm not sure why they were so slow to embrace technology in the first place—especially given the tech centers dotting the west coast—but the trial with Clan WildCanyon went well enough. So much so that the same system was rolled out to the entire Western Region."

Since Asher hadn't known Honoria would be one of the clan leader candidates, he hadn't researched her public information and only knew the bits and pieces of gossip floating around the clan. Before he could stop himself, he said, "That's quite impressive."

Honoria met his gaze, but he couldn't gauge her expression. That was a good point in her favor for the leadership trials. "It's one of the many things I hope to try in the UK. I learned a lot from my time in California. When humans stop fearing us so much, I think we should try exchanges between the clans. As it stands now, the dragon clans are too isolated, even with the ever-growing alliance between Stonefire and Lochguard."

Asher noticed her use of "when" and not "if" the humans stopped fearing dragon-shifters. She was more optimistic than he was. Especially given how more than a dozen dead bodies had been buried on Skyhunter's land not that long ago.

Of course, maybe things were different in northern California and her wish wasn't too extreme for clans without Skyhunter's dodgy past.

He raised an eyebrow. "I'm surprised you're telling me about your plans and ideas, given how we're rivals."

She never broke her gaze. "I think you're an honorable male and won't steal them."

As they stared at one another across the expanse of the kitchen, Asher suddenly wanted to know more about Honoria. She'd always been clever and adventurous, but he sensed she'd turned those traits into a useful set of skills as an adult.

Then he remembered his secrets and his living hell at the hands of the former leader. Asher may want to know more about Honoria, but she certainly wouldn't want to know everything about him. "I'm not the same dragonman you knew before you left, Ria. You'd best remember that."

He quickly turned to take out the biscuit tray, place it down as he turned off the oven, and strode out of the kitchen.

His dragon didn't waste time speaking up. *That was the most suspicious way to leave the room. Now Mum will pester us to no end.*

I don't care. Ria needs to remember a lot has changed over the years. If I allow her to believe I'm the same easygoing male from over a decade ago, it will only mislead her. Even if she's a rival, I don't want to do that with her.

His beast was silent a few beats before responding, *Then if you're not going to try to woo her into bed, can we do flight drills now?*

At the mention of flying, some of Asher's stress faded. His dragon had gone too many years without the freedom of the skies. *Of course.*

As they made their way toward the main landing area, Asher focused on making his dragon happy. Strengthening their bond would only help the both of them.

It was also the perfect distraction. Because images of Honoria's clear blue eyes and golden blonde hair kept filling his head.

And he could never let on to his inner dragon about how he thought the female had only become more beautiful with age. Because if his beast found out, Asher might eventually give in to his dragon's demands to sleep with her.

While he could withstand torture bringing him to the brink of death, it was harder to deny his dragon in certain areas. The top of the list was sex. Denying his beast sex put a strain on them both, and Asher hadn't been with a female since before his imprisonment.

Which meant if he wanted a fighting chance at the leadership trials, he needed to find a willing partner to tame his dragon's need. Only then could he focus harder on Asher's ultimate goal of winning. However, there was only one rule—the female needed to be anyone but Honoria Wakeham

Chapter Three

Even though Honoria had enjoyed sitting with Asher's mother and chatting over a good cuppa, her visit had brought more questions than answers.

Namely, she wondered who Asher King had become over the years.

Her dragon, now free again, spoke up. *I think we should talk to him one-on-one if you want to know the truth. Because of course he's going to be close-lipped around his mother when it comes to his recent past. Gossip says his sister was hurt, too, and who knows how badly. Talking of his experience would only increase his mum's sadness.*

She was debating how to respond when she spotted a large red dragon diving down and pulling up right before he hit the ground. It was only when he flew upward again that she saw his front and gasped.

A large K was branded into one side of his chest.

Scars in a dragon-shifter's human form usually translated into their dragon one as well. But to have such a scar told another story, namely that someone had rubbed certain toxins or dirt into the wound to keep it from healing. Or, he'd been burned. Badly. Dragon-shifters healed quickly, but not even the fastest healing dragonman or woman in the world could repair intense burns.

The red dragon reached its desired height and barrel-rolled back down to the earth. When he leaned to the side and changed direction at the last minute, Honoria recognized the move.

Asher had liked to show it off when they were younger, to win bets against the other teenage males.

Covering her mouth with her hand, Honoria's stomach rolled. Such a scar and its history was bad on anyone, but the thought of someone she'd once loved suffering such agony made her want to vomit.

Her beast spoke up. *We should find him and talk.*

About what? To bring up such a memory will only hurt him. Not only that, he'll think we're doing it on purpose to knock him off his game.

Didn't you notice how strained the flight maneuvers were and still are? Something is wrong with his dragon.

It could be Asher.

Or, it could be both.

She hesitated. The most common reasons for such strain was a lack of sex or concern about their mate. She'd learned that Asher didn't have a mate from his mother, so it had to be the former.

Her dragon hummed. *Yes, and we can help with it.*

As much as Honoria admired Asher's tall, muscled body, she was afraid such intimacy would stir something she didn't need. Or want, for that matter.

Her dragon grunted. *You're starting to sound like a human. Dragon-shifters need sex, end of story. I wouldn't mind a little release.*

Honoria teetered. In her opinion, she and Asher were the best candidates out of the group applying to be leader. Anything she could do to ensure they performed to the best of their abilities would be for the good of the clan.

Nodding, her dragon answered, *Exactly.*

Crap, she'd been projecting her private thoughts. *I'm going to be clear—one time, and that's it. After that, you stop bothering me about sex until after the clan leader trials are finished, and then work on focusing all your energy on winning.*

That will be difficult. I suspect Asher will be intense and dominating in bed. I'll want more than once.

The image of Asher above her, pinning her hands over her head as he teased between her legs flashed into her mind.

It'd been far too long since she'd had a male at the same dominance level—or higher—than her.

Her dragon chuckled. *You like that image.*

Not even Honoria could deny the sudden wetness between her thighs. *I'll allow multiple times during the same encounter, but no more. Winning and healing Skyhunter is too important to be distracted by a male.*

Her beast sighed. *Fine. But hurry up. Because of your naughty visions, all I can think of is Asher taking us from behind, making us moan his name, and squeezing his cock as we come.*

The image was clear as day in her mind, down to Asher slapping her arse once or twice as he murmured what he was going to do next. *Stop projecting that image into my head.*

I didn't. You're doing it yourself.

With a curse, Honoria picked up her pace and headed toward the main landing area. *Just be prepared because he may say no.*

Not if you kiss him first.

Such a randy dragon.

No more than any other.

Not wanting to argue the point, Honoria ignored her beast and half jogged to the landing area before she could change her mind. Sex *would* help, after all. She just needed to be smart about it.

~

Asher's breath was ragged when, in his dragon form, he touched his hind legs back on solid ground. Even though he was learning to be less self-conscious about the brand on one side of his chest, he preferred covering it than not, and began to shift so he could get dressed quickly.

Imagining his wings melding into his back, his tail retreating into his body, and his snout shrinking into a nose, he soon stood in his naked human form.

There were a few people coming and going, and quite a few were whispering. Whether because of his bloodlines or his brand, he didn't know since he routinely heard both. He reached the side of the landing area where small cubicles were carved out of the rock and took out his T-shirt. Asher had barely tugged it down when a familiar female voice came from behind him. "You've finessed what were once reckless drills into an art form."

Honoria had found him.

His dragon spoke up. *Maybe she wants what I want, so don't bother putting your boxers on.*

Asher did exactly that. Nudity was part of dragon-shifter life, but it wasn't just any dragon-shifter behind him. The last thing he needed was for his cock to go half- or full-mast and let the bloody female know how much he was still drawn to her.

Careful to keep his expression neutral, Asher turned around. Honoria was mere inches away, and as the wind blew, her delicious female scent invaded his senses.

His cock twitched to life. Yes, it was a good thing he had at least a little protection. He'd just need to make sure his dick didn't extend all the way to say hello.

Ignoring his dragon's cackles, he shrugged and replied, "If we'd had any other leader but the bastard we had, I would've become a Protector. Since I couldn't bring myself to support Marcus, I instead taught the young dragon-shifters how to fly properly."

"Even the moves you just did?"

He nodded. "I believe in fully preparing a child or teenager. A mutiny had been brewing right before I was imprisoned. I wanted to ensure the children could escape if chased, hoping they could make it to safety."

She studied his face. "I never would've pegged you as a teacher."

He shrugged. "Well, much like you, I suspect I found a more positive way to channel my adventurous and sometimes even reckless spirit."

Honoria arched one golden eyebrow. "I wasn't reckless."

The corner of his lips curled up, and Asher nearly blinked. It had been a long time since he'd smiled with anyone outside of his immediate family.

Quickly gathering his wits, he said, "I recall a female planning to fly across the Channel to France for a weekend, without any sort of approval from the DDA in either country."

She shook her head. "I didn't plan it out of nowhere. I only suggested it after we ran into those French dragon-shifters along the coast in Dover, who had done it first and were quite smug about it. Besides, you were helping me figure out how to pull it off. If not for my parents sending me away two weeks before our scheduled date, we would've tried it, too."

Over the years, Asher had had other things to worry about and think upon than his teenage girlfriend's disappearance. But standing in the landing area less than a foot away from Honoria, with the wind sending him her scent, the memory rushed back of when he'd learned how Honoria had been sent away. Before he could think better of it, he blurted, "No one discovered you had left for a week. It was only after I waited at our usual spot for half a day without any word from you that I thought something was wrong."

Asher paused, remembering the dread in his stomach back then. Even if he'd been a cocky teenage male who only thought he understood love, he'd cared about Honoria. And her missing their meeting had happened about the same time Marcus had started to use his policy of fear over diplomacy.

It had been a long few hours of figuring out what had happened to his girlfriend.

He continued, "So I went to your house, only to find two Protectors taking your parents away. Your mother saw me. She had tears in her eyes, and barely managed to say, 'Tell Honoria we love her,' before the Protector covered her mouth and carted her off."

Honoria's eyes looked suspiciously wet. "She said that?"

He nodded. "Yes."

They both knew what had come next. Marcus hadn't wanted anyone else to leave the clan, so he'd made an example out of Honoria's parents. At first they'd been imprisoned. But years later, as more people tried to send their children away, they'd been executed.

That had been the spark which made Asher join the secret faction wanting to overthrow Marcus King.

Honoria's voice was soft as she said, "Thank you for telling me that. I still blame myself to a degree, for not insisting I stay."

The strong, teasing female from earlier had disappeared. His dragon spoke up. *She is no different than us. We both have pain in our pasts.*

Asher debated what to do. He didn't sweet-talk females anymore, and he was afraid to comfort her with touch. Even something as simple as a hug could be too much for him.

Because as much as he may want to fight it, Asher wanted to hold Honoria in his arms once more. He could lie and say it was because he wanted closure on that chapter of his life. However, he wanted to hold her and see if the world simply felt right with her heat against him, like it had done in the past.

And if it did, that would complicate everything.

After wiping her eyes, Honoria smiled weakly. "Here I am about to cry, which is one of the unsexiest things in the world."

"Why is being sexy important? You are, of course, sexy. But it shouldn't matter."

Fuck. He definitely shouldn't have said that.

He expected a smile or even a chuckle. What he didn't expect was for Honoria's pupils to flash to slits and back, followed by pink spreading across her cheeks.

His beast spoke up. *I want to know why she's blushing. Maybe it's about us.*

I doubt it's about us. We just brought up the death of her parents.

Honoria's voice prevented any reply inside his mind. "So you still think I'm sexy. Good, then it's not one-sided and will make my proposition seem reasonable."

He frowned. "What the bloody hell are you talking about?"

"When was the last time you had sex, Ash?"

His dragon growled. *Almost six fucking years.*

Asher took a step back. "Why does that matter?"

"Are you really going to play this game? You and I are the strongest, most well-rounded candidates for clan leader."

"Yes, but—"

"So it makes sense that we should do everything possible to keep it that way and ensure we stay in the running." She took a step forward, but Asher didn't retreat. He'd barely acknowledged how nice it was not to have to look down at a female to meet her gaze when Honoria continued, "You need sex and so do I. I suggest we use each other to strengthen our chances at the trials."

He blinked. "What?"

"Release will make our dragons behave. Just one time, and then we each walk away and try our hardest to win the top spot."

His beast hummed. *Yes, yes, tell her yes.*

For a second, panic flared. He'd love nothing more than to slide between Honoria's thighs and fuck her senseless. However, he wasn't sure once would be enough. Even now, standing so close to her and feeling the heat of her body, he wanted to reach out and pull her close.

He'd never even slept with her as a teenager. What if doing so brought back feelings he didn't want, ones that could cost him the clan leadership?

His dragon grunted. *Us not fucking her will be more of a distraction. It's not like she's our true mate.*

As he tried to think of how to respond, Honoria took another step closer and placed a hand on his cheek. The touch sent a jolt of heat rushing through his body, straight to his cock. When she lightly caressed his skin, he barely resisted sighing and leaning into the touch.

A touch that seemed to soothe his soul.

Before he could think of why he shouldn't do it, Asher roped an arm around her waist, hauled her up against his body, and kissed her.

Honoria had been working up the courage to kiss Asher when he surprised her. The second her body pressed up against his, her knees buckled and she had to lean into him for support. Good thing, too, because in the next second he pressed his lips to hers.

A long-hidden desire rushed forth at the contact, her nerves aware of every inch of him against her. She opened her mouth and Asher thrust his tongue inside, caressing and stroking her breathless.

Bloody hell, he tasted good. Maybe even better than she remembered.

While not the pounding need of a mate-claim frenzy, Honoria wanted to kiss every inch of his body. Settling for touching his skin, she ran a hand under his shirt and dug her nails in. Asher growled at the contact, and he moved one of his hands to her arse. He rocked her against his hard cock, and she gasped.

She needed him inside her, and fast. He could rip off her clothes and take her right here, in the open, and she wouldn't care.

Asher broke the kiss, his breathing hard. He murmured, "Come on."

As he tugged her along, she smiled. "No adventurous sex today, I guess."

He never slowed down his pace. "I want to be the only one who sees your naked body as you come."

Heat flushed her body. "I hope not in your mother's house."

"No." He met her gaze. "A place where you can scream my name and no one will interrupt us. My place."

She frowned, thankful for her long legs being able to keep up with Asher's near-run. "You have a place?"

"Yes."

She sensed that was all the answer she'd get on the topic.

Her dragon spoke up. *It doesn't matter. He may want us to himself, but it's more that we have him to ourselves.*

They reached the front door of a small cottage made of brick, one in a different section of the clan from his mother's place. Asher unlocked the door, pulled her inside, and shut the door. She'd barely taken a glance at the sparsely furnished place before he backed her against the door and put a hand on either side of her head. His hot breath danced across her lips, a whisper of what she wanted. "Tell me you're on birth control."

Since dragon-shifters didn't catch venereal diseases, answering yes meant he'd be fucking her without a condom. The thought made her pussy pulse, so she didn't hide the truth and nodded.

He growled, "Good."

Asher kissed her and lifted her leg to his side. He wasted no time in reaching underneath and teasing her through her trousers. She gasped as his fingers found her clit.

But she wanted more than an orgasm brought on by his fingers. So Honoria broke the kiss, dug her nails into his chest, and pushed back. "No foreplay. I want you inside me. Now."

Her dragon hummed. *Yes, yes, he should fuck us hard and rough.*

Asher placed his hands over hers before encircling both her wrists. He maneuvered her hands behind her. "Any way I want?"

She knew her pupils were flashing between round and slitted, and her voice was husky as she answered, "Yes. Just hurry up and fuck me, Asher. It's been too long for me, too."

In the blink of an eye, Asher moved behind her and gently tugged her arms. Her dragon hummed at the dominance. *He isn't a weak one to cower at us. After the first orgasm, I'm not holding back.*

Keeping her wrists in place with one hand, he ripped her trousers until they pooled in tatters around her ankles. Her underwear was somehow also torn away in the process.

Moving his hand down, he teased her pussy. She sucked in a breath at his rough fingers against her swollen flesh. He murmured, "This isn't foreplay. But any male who doesn't ensure his female is wet and ready doesn't deserve to have a cock."

Somewhere in her lust haze, she realized Asher was still an honorable male. That hadn't changed.

Removing his fingers, he pushed her forward to a small sofa, and he bent her over the back. "If it's ever too much, you say bonanza. Understood?"

Honoria wiggled her hips and widened her stance. Between his heat behind her and the way he wasn't afraid to take charge, she needed his hard cock. "Bonanza. Yes, I got it. Now, fuck me."

There was no teasing, no joking. Asher positioned his cock at her entrance and pushed in an inch. One bloody inch. "Bloody hell, Asher. Just fuck me already."

She swore she heard a chuckle, but he thrust into her with one swift motion and she arched her back. "Asher."

He remained that way, deep inside her, keeping her arms restrained, for a few seconds. She should be frustrated, but more wetness rushed between her thighs in anticipation of what he'd do next.

So this was what it was like to be taken by a dominant male.

Her beast snarled. *I am just as dominant. The next round is mine.*

Asher moved his hips, his long, hard cock hitting just the right spot. The sofa even moved beneath her from the force of his thrusts.

The dragonman behind her reached an arm around her and lightly brushed her clit. A few more harsh strokes and Honoria was close to coming.

Lights danced before her eyes as the world broke apart. Pleasure exploded throughout her body, both the human and dragon roaring in ecstasy. She was vaguely aware of Asher stilling and grunting out his own orgasm.

Their heavy breathing filling the air, Honoria slowly came back to her surroundings. Her dragon spoke up. *No one else has ever come close. I want him again.*

Asher gently pulled her up and kissed the side of her neck. He lazily ripped her top off. Her bra soon followed. Taking one of her hard nipples between thumb and forefinger, he rolled and tugged, making her want him all over again.

Her dragon snarled. *Yes, yes, again. But this time, it's my turn.*

With her beast taking control of her mind, she freed her arms, batted away Asher's hand, and turned. "I will claim you now."

Her beast rushed Asher and took him to the ground. Turning one of their fingernails into a talon, she put it at his throat. Taking his cock in other hand, she stroked. "Have you had a dominant female before?"

His pupils were slitted. "No."

She smiled slowly. "Good. Then this should be fun."

Her dragon lowered their body onto his cock and clenched their inner muscles. Asher groaned and tilted his head back. Her beast dug the talon deeper. "Look at me." Asher complied. "And don't stop."

Moving their hips, her dragon rode Asher hard. His gaze never wavered, not even when they both orgasmed shortly after.

And even then, it wasn't enough for either woman or beast. It wasn't just great sex either. There was something about Asher that affected her greatly, to the point it should set off warning bells.

However, as he took her again, Honoria forgot about everything but the male inside her.

Hours later, Asher lay on his back on the floor, Honoria a few inches away from him. They'd both taken turns dominating the other, until exhaustion had reduced them to lying like logs on the floor.

Never had Asher thought giving up control could be as sexy as it had been with Honoria.

His dragon sniffed. *It only is with the* right *female.*

In other words, one who lets us dominate her sometimes, too.

Exactly. We're tied two-two, which means we need to schedule a rematch.

No, dragon. This is a one-time thing. We should both be more levelheaded and focused on the clan leader trials now.

If not for the trials, you'd want her again, wouldn't you?

Asher turned his head a fraction and stared at Honoria's profile. While he would never tire of her small breasts or long legs, it was her face he couldn't look away from. Much like he, she had a light sheen of sweat on her forehead. There were also a few nips on her neck that were beginning to bruise. And her lovely hair was tangled, but he knew it was still soft and faintly smelled of some kind of fruit.

He'd once called her the most beautiful female in the world. That hadn't changed.

Honoria turned her head and met his gaze. A small smile played on her lips as she said, "I'm almost glad we didn't do this at sixteen. Because I suspect your teenage dragon wouldn't have let mine take control part of the time."

"Maybe not."

She snorted. "Which is dragonman talk for never."

He smiled. Honoria had a way of making him do that. "Teenage dragon-shifters are fools half the time. Anyone who spends time teaching them learns that soon enough."

She searched his gaze. "Have you been teaching again since being let out?"

He looked away. His beast murmured, *Coward.*

Ignoring his dragon, Asher whispered, "A little."

Her hand found his and squeezed. Rationally, he should jerk his hand away and keep a distance between them. Sex was one thing, but sharing more of him could only lead to trouble later on.

And yet, he squeezed her fingers back. With her warm hand in his, the usual dread that came when talking about his past seemed to stay at bay.

His dragon grunted. *Talk to her.*

Why? She's not ours, and never will be.

She could be.

Not allowing himself to think of Honoria in his bed every night, pulled close against him, Asher focused on Skyhunter. Any good clan leader would do the same. "Teaching was great, but leading the clan back into the light and earning the trust of Stonefire and the other clans will be even more rewarding." He did meet her lovely blue eyes again. "I've spent the last six months dedicating myself to taming my demons."

"And did you succeed?"

He should scream yes and be done with it. However, the words spilled from his lips, "Mostly. Enough to be declared sane and stable by the counselor, at any rate."

He paused, debating whether to say more. Then Honoria gripped his hand tighter, and he couldn't resist the comforting gesture. When it came to the female next to him, Asher had a definite weakness. He added, "But unlike most other leaders, I plan to have a better structure in place surrounding the clan leader, to ensure nothing like Marcus's reign of terror happens ever again. I would be in charge, yes. But I'd also have others working with me on various tasks and specialties to better distribute the workload."

Honoria's eyes widened and her lips parted. "That just sparked an idea."

"Which is?"

She bit her bottom lip, and Asher somehow resisted moving over and kissing her again. He instead focused on her response as she said, "You aren't going to like it."

He raised an eyebrow. "And you think saying that is going to make me shrug and drop it?"

Smiling, amusement danced in her eyes. Honoria had such beautiful blue eyes. Ones he could easily lose himself in if Asher weren't careful.

His dragon huffed. *Stop being poetic and just fuck her again.*

Honoria spoke before he could reply to his dragon. "Well, the UK and Ireland have been pushing boundaries and trying new things in their clans over the last few years, right?" He nodded, and she continued, "What would you say to pushing a boundary even further?'

He frowned. "You're being cryptic. Just spit it out, Ria."

Releasing his hand, she sat up and motioned for him to do the same. Once he was upright, it was harder to keep his eyes on her face. But somehow he managed it as she spoke again, "What if Skyhunter had *two* clan leaders, working together? Sort of like co-leaders, you could say. After all, you know Skyhunter better than anyone, and I have knowledge gained from my time in America concerning some of the most modern practices between dragons and human oversight. If we combine those things, as well as our other numerous strengths, we could make Skyhunter respected once again, and this time not out of fear."

He blinked. "Two clan leaders? Has that ever been done before?"

She shrugged one shoulder. "I have no idea, but does it matter? I know it's going to be hard to convince not only the DDA of how it could work, but also the other four dragon clan leaders in the UK. However, I think we could do so much together, Ash. More than either of us could on our own."

He stared at Honoria. The idea wasn't bad, but it also raised other important issues.

His beast spoke up. *So you're open to it?*

She has a point.

And it has nothing to do with seeing her sparkling eyes every day?

Asher mentally grunted. *It would be a bonus, but it's not the main reason.*

However, as he searched Honoria's gaze, he wondered if he truly knew what she was proposing. "It's a good idea." She opened her mouth, but he raised a hand to stay her and continued, "But I haven't agreed to anything. Everyone will talk, Ria. They'll think we're together, and many of them will still think the male of the pair is ultimately in charge. Could you handle that?"

She sat up taller. "They may assume that in the beginning, but with time, they'll learn that certain areas are my jurisdiction, and others are yours."

The bold girl from his youth had blossomed into a confident female, one he wanted to haul into his lap and claim all over again.

His beast snorted. *If you're thinking about a platonic relationship, I don't think it'll last.*

It'll last because it has to.

Want to wager on it?

No.

Only because you know you'll lose.

"Ash? Is your dragon against the idea?"

He shook his head. "No. He's just being a smug pain in my arse, is all."

She grinned. "So in other words, just a male dragon?"

His beast cackled inside his head, but Asher ignored him. "He's the only dragon I have, so I don't know."

Searching his gaze, she leaned forward. "So? What do you think?"

There were a million reasons why he should dismiss Honoria's idea and earn the clan leader position on his own.

And yet, just imagining Honoria always nearby, ready to take charge if something triggered a flashback to his torture, was too irresistible. Especially since she would have a hard time winning over the older clan members on her own. Not everyone was as open to a female leader as Clan Glenlough in Ireland.

His beast grunted. *Honoria's entirely capable and skilled.*

I don't disagree. But our stubbornness won't instantly change everyone's minds.

He finally answered Honoria's question. "I'm open to it." She squealed in delight, but he carried on. "But it's not ultimately up to me, Ria. We have to convince the DDA to allow it, which won't be easy."

She grabbed his hand, her warm skin against his making him want to kiss her again. "No worries, we can do it. I know we can, Ash. We need to schedule a private meeting with the DDA human as soon as possible. Where's my phone?"

He finally pulled her closer and rearranged her on his lap. "You can call them after we have our tie-breaking match."

"Ash, we shouldn't waste time."

His hand moved to between her thighs, and he lightly stroked her folds. He groaned at how wet she still was. "Cede to me straightaway and it won't take long."

Her pupils flashed to slits and back. Instead of speaking, she pushed him back and raised herself to her knees while straddling him. "I don't think so."

With his hard cock in hand, she lowered down and began riding him rough, digging her nails into his chest as she swirled her hips.

He should be upset at losing, but as Honoria gripped his cock with her pussy and increased her pace, he said fuck it. Sometimes, losing wasn't so bad. Especially when Honoria Wakeham was involved.

Chapter Four

The following day, Asher sat next to Honoria in what was usually the clan leader's office. For the time being, the human DDA employee was using it as her home base.

It was strange to see a human sitting behind the massive desk that had been used for centuries by Skyhunter's leaders. Some may think it should be destroyed, to cleave all ties to Marcus King's reign. However, Asher thought keeping the desk and sitting behind it to do good would be better. Most of Skyhunter's past wasn't so dark, after all. There were even times in history, such as during the Second World War, when they'd been viewed as heroes.

Not that he should be thinking about the desk at all. Honoria had just finished telling Penny about her co-leader idea, and they awaited her response. The human kept looking at each of them in turn, her brows furrowed, clearly thinking.

When she finally spoke, her voice was firm. For a human, at least. "Part of me wants to outright dismiss the request since Skyhunter will face enough challenges with just one new leader."

At her pause, Asher jumped in. "I sense a 'but' coming."

Penny sat back in her chair and sighed. "But, it could

be a good thing, too. After all, having two dragon-shifters working together, not to mention the additional support staff you propose, would severely decrease the chance of corruption. It could still happen, mind you. But it'd be less likely, given all the dragon-shifters involved in keeping the clan running."

Honoria tapped her hand against the arm of her chair. Asher remembered her having the same tick when she'd been younger, and it was the only sign she was anxious to hear a verdict. The dragonwoman asked, "So may we compete as a pair?"

"The others will no doubt make a fuss. We'd have to extend the chance for them to compete as a team, too." She looked at each of them. "Do you still want to do this?"

They both nodded, but Honoria spoke first. "Of course."

"Right, then I need to call my boss first and then Stonefire."

Asher's brows drew together. "Why do you need to talk with Stonefire?"

The human answered, "They are the other English dragon clan, and probably the one you'll be working with the most closely. It's essential you two get along. Given what I know of Bram Moore-Llewellyn, it shouldn't be a problem. However, I need to clear it with him first."

It was on the tip of Asher's tongue to say fuck Stonefire, but he held back.

His dragon spoke up. *You'd better. And while I know you hate having others in charge of your fate thanks to what Marcus did, Bram is different. Everything we've read about him says he's a good bloke, and he doesn't want to control everyone.*

Maybe. But you also know that Stonefire has been steering a lot of the changes in the UK whilst we were imprisoned. Who's to say they won't try to change things here, too?

We'll be meeting him soon enough. Save judgment until after you can interact with him in person.

Since Asher had been talking with his dragon, he'd missed Honoria's question. But the human spoke again. "I'll have an answer for you tomorrow. The next stage of the leadership trials won't be for a few days anyway, so if you can compete as a team, you'll know before then. Now, if you'll excuse me, I have loads to do in the next few hours."

Standing, Asher exited the office and Honoria followed. Only once they were outside the cottage used by most of the former clan leaders did Asher speak again. "I don't like other clans having a say in what we do."

Honoria rolled her eyes. "They were going to play a part in choosing Skyhunter's leader anyway, so I don't see the big deal." Her expression softened. "Besides, how much do you know of Stonefire's leader?"

He shrugged one shoulder. "Not much, only what I could read. I've never met him. However, judging from what I've absorbed, he's had a lot of sway with the DDA for the last few years."

"Not exactly true. His mate is a former DDA employee, and she has a lot of contacts. Not to mention the human mate of another dragonman wrote a book which helped humans see us as more than monsters. And then there's the other human mate who has a videocast series introducing aspects of dragon-shifter life to the general public. If anything, the humans of Stonefire are doing a lot of the influencing."

"How do you know all this, Ria? You weren't even in the country."

Honoria had wanted to leave the cottage and propose a joint training session with Asher. However, he voiced his doubts and then asked her how she knew so much about Bram and Stonefire.

Asher's tone hadn't been accusatory, just curious. It was the only reason she hadn't scowled and pulled him into an abandoned building to give him a scolding.

The downside to potentially being a co-leader team was that they needed to project trust and cohesion in public. If she needed to chew his arse out, it would have to be done in private.

Her dragon spoke up. *Good. Then it gives me a chance to take control and give him a lesson my way.*

Ignoring her beast, she replied to Asher's questions, "Just because I was thousands of miles away doesn't mean I didn't keep track of what was happening back in the UK. Even though my parents are dead, I'd still hoped to return at some point."

"If not for the trials, would you have come?"

She looked into the distance, studying the softly rolling hills that surrounded Skyhunter on most sides. England was so much greener than back in Northern California. "Yes, although maybe not this soon." She looked back to Asher. "I still have some family in the UK, after all."

Her English cousins had gone to the Northern Irish clan and still hadn't returned to Skyhunter.

Her dragon spoke up. *We can invite them back once we're in charge. Surely they'll trust us to keep everything in line.*

I hope so. It'd be nice to have more family nearby.

Don't tell me you miss our cousins in America? They bloody annoyed us to no end.

Maybe. But they stood at our side when we needed it.

Namely, when Honoria had first arrived and had wanted

to do nothing more than cry, her cousins had done their best to tease her and irritate her, all to help her forget her pain.

Her dragon huffed. *I'm still not convinced that was the reason.*

Asher's voice cut into her thoughts. "Right, then if we're to work together, maybe you should help me catch up with information about Bram and the other leaders. I don't want my lack of knowledge to be the reason we fail."

"I can do that, but you're going to teach me those flight maneuvers you did earlier in return."

The corner of his mouth ticked up. "If you think you can manage them, that is. I can't have you crashing into the ground."

She raised an eyebrow. "I can handle it, and then some. I have a few tricks of my own."

"Good, then it means I won't have to go easy on you."

Honoria was about to throw down a challenge, but the voice of Shane Farhall filled the air. "What's this I heard about you two teaming up and cheating?"

Taking a deep breath, she turned around at the same time Asher did. Hoping to avoid any sort of confrontation, she spoke before Asher could. "It's not cheating, Shane. You have the same chance as anyone else, and can compete with a partner."

Shane scowled. "If Skyhunter has two leaders, it'll broadcast to the world how we're weak. Especially since every other clan on the planet has only one person in charge."

Asher grunted. "And you've talked with every other clan in the world? Last I heard, the clans in New Zealand and Peru were refusing to talk to anyone at all. They could be having mass orgies every day there, and we'd never know it."

Honoria couldn't help but add, "Unless it's truly everyone participating in the orgies, then it might show up on the satellite images."

Asher snorted, but Shane took a step closer and growled. "You're not bloody funny, bitch. Stop trying to be like the wankers in the north and in Scotland. Humor is a sign of weakness, as it usually means the person in question can't fight properly."

"And you know this how?" she drawled.

Shane took a step toward her, but Asher stepped in the way and shoved him back. "No fighting, unless you want to be thrown out of the trials."

"If it means she's out too, then it might just be worth it," Shane spat.

Her dragon sighed. *Does he think he's being macho or something?*

Maybe. Remember, Marcus was our leader for a good chunk of his life. And under that dragonman, fear and a projection of strength were all that mattered.

Her beast grunted. *Let me have a go. I bet he's a coward when it comes to an actual fight.*

Asher crossed his arms over his chest, but still stayed in front of Honoria. She was tempted to step in front of him and handle Shane herself. But if they were to work together, she needed to admit Asher would be better in certain situations. It was clear Shane didn't respect females. Asher could probably get him to walk away easier than she could, and without her being tossed out of the contest, too.

Asher spoke up. "In previous trials, leader candidates have been kept apart and in seclusion for the entire duration, unless they were competing in an event. Either leave us alone, or I'll request it from the DDA. That means fixed quarters, no freedom to practice in the skies, and no chance to visit that girlfriend of yours, either."

"Asher," she whispered.

Her beast said, *After being imprisoned for so long and to be willing to temporarily lose his freedom again speaks volumes about his character. It makes me want him again. Many times. He would be a fine mate.*

Shane's reply prevented her from saying anything to her dragon. "No one wants to risk being tossed into a cell and never being let out again. Everyone would hate you and see it as a sign that you're just like your uncle."

Asher shrugged. "Either agree to leave us alone or I'll call the DDA human right now."

For a few beats, Shane just kept glaring at Asher. But when he turned half away, Honoria knew Shane would back down. The male gave him the double-finger salute and said, "Fuck you, King. You'll lose anyway. I'll team up with another male, and then you'll understand how working with a female puts you at a huge disadvantage."

The male walked away, his fingers clenched into fists. Her dragon shook her head. *Once we win, remind me to challenge him to a series of flight maneuvers. Then he'll see how much of a burden we are.*

Leave it, dragon. My guess is that Shane will flee Skyhunter if he loses. And he will lose.

Someone's confident.

Bluster can only get you so far, and I'm sure the other leaders will see through it. At least Bram and Finn will.

Speaking of which, we should thank Asher for getting Shane off our arses. Maybe a few times. And then we can focus on training him up.

She ignored her beast and touched Asher's bicep. "I'm grateful for your help, but I hope you understand that I'm not going to always sit back and let you protect me."

Uncrossing his arms, Asher faced her. "Of course not. But Shane thinks females are only good for fucking and bearing babies, and nothing else. He might have risked being tossed out of the trials if it meant you were out, too. I couldn't risk it. I promise, the next arsehole we come across, he's all yours."

She snorted. "You're so confident that it'll be a male."

"Well, dragon-shifters skew more male than female, so statistically, it's likely."

"Okay, mister smarty-pants, are you done?"

He raised an eyebrow. "America has definitely rubbed off on you, Ria."

She shrugged and put on a mock accent. "I could be, like, totally cool, and like, talk like this all day to totes annoy you."

Asher chuckled. "You'd probably tire of it before me."

Her dragon laughed. *He's right.*

Not wanting to acknowledge the point to either her dragon or Asher, she motioned toward the path. "Let me tell you more about Bram and Stonefire, and then you can teach me a few flight drills."

"If I show you my secret moves, will you cook me something special, too?"

"Maybe I don't cook anymore." He raised his brows and she smiled. "Okay, I do. Although it's mostly Chinese, Japanese, or Korean. All of those are popular and quite tasty in San Francisco." Honoria should leave it at that, but something inside of her added, "But only if you help me prepare everything. That way you can learn at the same time, and then you'll cook for me later."

Once the words left her lips, she had no idea how Asher would respond. He'd gone on about being careful and keeping distance between them.

And yet, the longer she was around him, the more Honoria wanted to get to know him better. No, he wasn't her true mate, but that didn't mean they wouldn't fit together. After all, the female leader in Ireland had mated a dragonman who wasn't her true mate, and all sorts of reports floated around of them being in love and perfect for each other.

Maybe she'd come back to Skyhunter for more than helping the clan. Maybe she'd known her future mate since she'd been a child.

Not wanting to think about it, she prompted Asher, "Well, what's your answer to my deal? Or, are you afraid of a little work and touching some seafood?"

"I'm not afraid." He put out his hand. "Come on. I want to get as much done as possible before someone else bothers us."

Slipping her hand into his, a sizzle of heat shot up her arm at the contact. Even though she'd had Asher five times the day before, she burned to tear off his clothes and make it a sixth and seventh time, too.

Her dragon spoke up. *Then do it.*

We can't, until maybe later.

So you are thinking about him naked again. Good, because I want to ride him hard. Maybe even tie his arms up once.

Whoa, slow down. We can't forget about the trials and preparing for them. Let's wait until after dinner.

While now would be better, I suppose I can wait until then.

Her beast fell silent, and Honoria tried not to think about how she'd just agreed to wanting more sex with Asher. So much for her one-time-only resolve.

CHAPTER FIVE

Asher lazily flapped his wings to maintain his altitude and watched as Honoria dove toward the earth.

It was her second attempt. The first one had resulted in her almost smacking into the ground and doing serious damage.

His dragon spoke up. *I still can't believe you wanted to tell her to stop. Then she would've tried it on her own, whether we were nearby or not.*

Ignoring his beast, he held his breath as Honoria barreled down, her wings pressed flat against her white dragon form. There wasn't much sun, but he remembered from his youth how her scales were more iridescent in the sunshine than white.

She was beautiful in any form.

His dragon snorted, but then it came time for Honoria to pull up and his beast moved their dragon head forward to watch.

One, two, three...and Honoria released her wings and maneuvered her body so that the currents swerved her up toward the sky again.

He let out his breath and said to his beast, *She's still a fast learner, and more skilled than I had assumed.*

All the males probably think the same. 'She is female, so she must be weak' is the traditional way of thinking.

Asher didn't like imagining others who would dismiss Honoria so easily. *It just means we have to win this thing and prove everyone wrong.*

To do that, we need to be at our best. I think showing Ria a thing or two with our cock will energize her right up.

If he would've been in his human form, Asher would've smiled. *You tell her that and see what happens.*

Honoria hovered in front of them, flapping her wings to stay in place. She tilted her head in question, and Asher didn't hesitate to bob his in acknowledgment, letting her know she'd done it correctly.

Since his promise had been teaching her one tough maneuver before they ended the session, he pointed toward the ground with his hind leg, then to her, and back to the ground again. Trusting her to understand, he dove toward the landing area.

A long-held need to impress surged through Asher's body and he pressed his wings against his back so that he fell faster toward the ground. When he was near enough to the landing area, he released his wings, held firm against the sudden jolt of resistance, and then glided the remainder of the distance to the ground. The second he touched his hind legs to the earth, the sound of clapping filled the air.

Looking over his shoulder, Asher spotted a group of dragon-shifters mostly in their late teens and early twenties. It took him a second to recognize them; they were some of his former students. All grown and no doubt less innocent than when he'd last seen them, but as he looked at each of their faces, they only had smiles and approval for him.

His dragon said softly, *Let's shift and talk with them. They won't blame you for abandoning them, I'm positive.*

One of the many things Asher had worried about during his imprisonment was if his students would be safe. He'd tried to teach them how to flee if necessary, but he'd never been certain if it'd been enough.

His dragon spoke again. *Whilst not all of our former students are here, many are. Let's find out what happened. If we're to ever be leader, we need to start showing everyone that we are healed and ready.*

Since Asher had spent the last six months trying to heal himself and tackle his demons, he'd steered clear of almost everyone who wasn't his mother and sister. For the first time, he felt confident saying, *I think we* are *ready to talk with them.*

Asher imagined his wings shrinking into his back, his forearms and hind legs shortening, and his snout morphing back into a nose and mouth.

Once he stood in his human form, the group of former students rushed toward him. One of the older boys—correction, Tony was now a young adult male—was first to speak. "That was brilliant, Mr. Asher. I vaguely remember seeing those maneuvers back when you were teaching, but either you're better now or my memory is crap."

A female not much younger than him snickered. "It's your memory, Tony."

Tony glared, but Asher noticed the look turned into one of love. He suspected the pair were an item.

Another male spoke up. "Tony, I think it's a bit of both, if I'm being honest. You always had a hard time memorizing facts or protocols, even if you are a genius with numbers."

Another female spoke up, one who had to be in her midteens and couldn't have been more than nine or ten when Asher had last seen her. "Mr. Asher, is it true you're vying to be our new clan leader?"

He was vaguely aware of Honoria walking up to them in her human form, completely dressed. He glanced over his shoulder and raised an eyebrow in question. Did she want him to tell the group about the joint venture?

The second she nodded, Asher looked back at the younger dragon-shifters. “I am, but not by myself. Honoria and I are running as a team.”

Murmurs raced through the group, but it was the girl who’d asked about him running who managed to speak first. “I’ve never heard of two people wanting to lead a clan together before.”

His beast said, *See how she didn’t first pounce on Honoria being a female? That’s a good sign.*

Honoria answered the female, “It’s uncommon. And I don’t know enough of other clan histories to say if it’s ever been done at all. However, Asher and I think it’s a good idea.” She winked. “After all, female dragon-shifters usually avoid going to war or other such violent measures more often than the males. That alone is a point in my favor.”

One of the younger males snorted. “Maybe, but I’ve read a lot of stories about female dragon-shifters poisoning each other. That’s just as bad.”

His dragon laughed. *He’s read one too many books.*

Asher focused on the male. “Honoria isn’t going to poison anyone, just like I’m not going to start a war with anyone. We all know firsthand what a rotten leader is like, and I vow to never be one.”

Silence fell over the group. Maybe Asher should’ve tiptoed around the issue, but doing so long term wouldn’t help the clan. They need to acknowledge the former leader’s reign, talk about it, and begin to heal and move on.

Honoria lightly touched his back, and he took comfort from it. “I know you won’t be like that, Ash.”

One of the females spoke up. "Me, too, Mr. Asher. You always went out of your way to show how even those of us who are a bit weaker and slower than usual could flee, if needed. You always cared about all of us."

The group of his former students all murmured something similar. And for the first time, Asher truly believed there was hope for Skyhunter.

His beast spoke up. *Their belief is only the beginning. Others will follow, especially as we progress through the trials.*

Asher liked the fact his dragon was confident, without being overly so.

One of the younger males spoke up. "We'll be cheering you on, Mr. Asher. And maybe someday, you can teach us a few more of your tricks. Not that we'll need them if you and your partner win, but it'd be nice to learn them all the same. After all, the dragon hunters or Dragon Knights could come down south at any time."

So far, both enemies had mostly focused on Stonefire and Lochguard to the north. However, Asher worried about them coming to Skyhunter and possibly sweet-talking some of the more vulnerable clan members into helping them, especially if they rejected a dual leadership if he and Honoria won.

His beast grunted. *If they work with anyone out to drain dragon-shifters of their blood, then maybe they're too stupid to live.*

A clan leader can't protect only the intelligent. Part of our job will be to watch out for the most vulnerable.

His dragon huffed. *I'm sure in the days of old they banished the weaker ones from the clan in order to survive.*

You don't really mean that.

No, although if we don't eat soon, I'm going to get even grumpier and propose more old-fashioned traditions.

Not dignifying his cranky dragon with a response, he glanced around the group of former students. "If things ever settle down enough, I'll hold some special training days in the future. But just know that there is a lot to do before things will probably settle down here."

One of the females bobbed her head. "I know, Mr. Asher. But we'll be waiting all the same."

Asher made his goodbyes and followed Honoria. Once they were out of earshot, she spoke up again. "Well, at least we know not everyone will dismiss me working with you."

"I'm sure others will approve, and hopefully more will follow. But first, we need to be as prepared as we can be. So let's hurry up to your place so you can catch me up on everything I missed."

Honoria nodded. "We'll go, but I propose a race. The last one to my place has to shell and devein the shrimp?"

He was about to say he didn't know where she lived now, but Honoria was already running away. All Asher could do was grab his clothes, tug them on, and follow.

Even though Honoria had cheated, he smiled the whole way to her cottage, and even more so when he finally caught up to her. It'd been a while since he'd had to chase a female, and Asher forgot how much he liked it.

Maybe it'd been childish to suggest a race—especially one to a location Asher didn't know about—but Honoria had wanted to win and make Asher clean up the shrimp for dinner. And so she ran as fast as she could, Asher's footsteps behind her telling her he wasn't far behind.

Her dragon spoke up. *Yes, yes, I like the chase.*

He's not chasing us, dragon.

Are you sure? He could eat anywhere. And maybe even find out more about Stonefire and Lochguard on his own, too. No, he's chasing us.

You're turning into a one-track mind sort of dragon, aren't you?

Her beast grunted. *Only because you do the human thing and deny what we both want.*

I said I wanted him, but not yet.

Sex on a schedule isn't sexy.

Thankfully Honoria's little stone cottage came into view, and she pushed her body harder. Reaching the front step, she turned. Asher was in front of her in the next second. With him standing a step below, she was a fraction taller than him, and Honoria admitted she liked it when he was a smidge taller than her since most males were shorter than her.

As if reading her mind, Asher moved onto the same step, all but pressing her into the door. His hot breath danced across her face, his body less than an inch away from hers.

For a second, they merely stared at one another, breathing hard—from the running, most definitely because of the running. Not because Asher was so close, his heat enveloping her like a coat.

Her dragon growled. *Lying again.*

Asher's voice was low as he said, "Open the door, Ria. Now."

She fished the keys from her bra and turned toward the door. The position made it so her back was up against Asher's front. Heat blazed where he touched her despite their clothing, and she expected him to wrap an arm around her waist or maybe kiss her neck.

But all he did was stand there, waiting.

Not wanting him to think he should always be giving the orders, Honoria deliberately pushed her arse back until she could feel his hard cock. With a little wiggle, she made Asher growl, "Open the fucking door, Ria."

Glancing over her shoulder, she threw back, "Patience is a necessary virtue for clan leaders, isn't it?"

Asher reached around, and since she'd put the key in the lock, he turned it, pushed the door open and backed her inside. He didn't hesitate to shut the door and press her up against it, his arms caging her body. His strained voice filled the hall. "I was showing bloody patience by not turning you around and kissing you out in the open."

Her heart kicked up, and her eyes fell to his lips. "You wanted to kiss me?"

He moved a fraction closer. "Lately, I always bloody want to kiss you. But if we're to be a clan leader team, it's probably best if we keep any kissing private."

Her eyes shot back to his. "So no platonic relationship, then?"

His pupils flashed to slits and back. "Originally, I had thought of it. But, fuck, Ria, every time you're near, something happens to my brain and I can't think straight."

She smiled. "Well, that tends to happen when the blood heads south."

He growled. "No, no teasing. Unless it's the kind I can do with my tongue and teeth."

Memories of Asher licking between her thighs flashed inside her mind, and her dragon spoke up. *Yes, yes, let's fuck him now. Dinner can wait till later.*

Without being in public and everyone watching them, Honoria stopped denying what she wanted. She lifted a hand to his chest and tilted her head. "I could be your snack before supper, if you want."

Asher took her lips in a rough kiss, his tongue thrusting into her mouth as one hand moved into her hair. Honoria wrapped her arms around his neck as she twined and stroked her tongue with his, giving back to Asher as good as she got.

Her beast hummed. *I want more than kissing. Tell him, now, or I'll take control.*

You bloody won't this time. Try, and I'll put you in a mental prison.

Her dragon fell silent, and Honoria focused on kissing Asher as she ran one hand down his back, to his arse, and then around to his front. When she cupped his balls, he groaned. "Keep that up and I'm not going to be able to hold back and worship your pussy with my tongue."

She squeezed again. "The tongue can wait."

Asher's pupils turned to slits and back as he extended a few talons and shredded her jeans. She squeaked. "Hey, you need to stop ripping my clothes. I don't have a lot of them here yet."

"You don't need any inside the house," he threw back as he shucked his own clothes.

She opened her mouth, but then her eyes fell to Asher's hand, which pumped his cock as he closed in on her.

Her beast spoke up. *Yes, yes, knock him down and take him. I want him now. No more waiting.*

In that moment, Honoria decided that in the confines of her own home, she would go after what she wanted. And right now, what she wanted was Asher King inside her and making her scream.

Honoria tugged off the remaining bits of her clothing and walked over to her sofa. But unlike last time, she sat on the back of it before he could bend her over. Not that she didn't like it, but she wanted to watch his eyes as he took her.

Spreading her legs wide, Honoria played with her pussy and then her clit. Asher watched every moment, his hand pumping faster.

Her dragon grunted. *Tell him to stop or he'll only last a minute or two. I want longer, much longer. He needs to prove he can hold out.*

Why? That isn't a clan leader requirement.

It is for me, if he's ever to be our mate.

Honoria tried to digest her dragon's words, but Asher was in front of her, gripping her hand and moving it away. She quickly added to her beast, *We'll talk about that later.*

Asher's deep voice rolled over her. "Stop talking with your bloody dragon and stay with me."

He rubbed the tip of his dick against her, and Honoria sucked in a breath. Somehow she had enough of her mind left to say, "Don't think you can order me about all the time, Asher King."

"You? Never." He placed the tip of his cock inside her. "Your dragon, on the other hand? I plan to test her boundaries all the bloody time."

Her dragon growled, but then Asher thrust into Honoria and moved his hips. To keep from falling backward, she held onto his arms, making sure to dig in her nails. "Just shut up and kiss me."

He snorted. "And now who's giving the orders?"

Pulling out slowly, Asher thrust back in hard as he took her lips with his, swallowing her reply. Maybe she should be a little angry, but as he moved and pulled her close, she forgot about everything but Asher's tongue battling hers, his cock claiming her core, and his hands roaming, caressing, and pulling her close.

Maybe a future with Asher wouldn't be such a bad idea after all.

Then his fingers found her clit, and any remaining shreds of thought vanished as he rubbed and pressed, playing her like an expert. Each pass sent her closer to the edge, making her moan with a few whimpers. Asher was inside her, around her, invading all of her senses. And when she finally crashed over the edge and wave after wave of pleasure flooded her body, she couldn't help but murmur his name into his mouth, instantly craving him all over again.

In a way she'd never craved another male before.

Asher stilled and held her closer as he broke the kiss and bit her neck. "Ria," he whispered, the tension draining from his body as he came.

Honoria laid her head on his shoulder and hugged him tightly. Asher's voice had been more than a response to his orgasm. His tone had been filled with awe, as well as need. It'd almost sounded like he'd been waiting for her all these years.

Which was ridiculous, of course. So she merely held him in her arms and tried not to think of how he'd been the male she'd once loved and could easily love again.

CHAPTER SIX

Three days later, Asher looked down at Honoria's sleeping face and wondered how he ever thought he could be around her and not touch her.

His dragon spoke up. *She wants us to touch her. That's all that matters.*

He wanted to say it wasn't, but he and his beast had argued the last three days about how bad of an idea it'd be if they became a true couple, won the contest, and then something went wrong.

His beast huffed. *You don't have enough faith. I don't want to give her up. I will fight for her. You should want to do it, too.*

Honoria moved her head against the pillow and shifted the position of her arm. But after a few beats, Asher deemed her still asleep and he replied, *The clan needs to come first right now.*

Before his dragon could say anything, Asher's phone beeped with a message. He looked and read it: *You and Honoria's next appointment is at 10:00 a.m. at the Protector building.*

He mentally cursed. It was nearly nine o'clock now, which meant he had to wake Honoria. Yet as he stared at her face slack in sleep, her hair half covering it, he wanted to let her rest after keeping her up half the night.

His dragon snorted. *More like she kept* us *up half the night.*

Ignoring his beast, he gently tucked some of her long, blonde hair behind her ear and lightly traced her cheek. "Ria, wake up." When she didn't move, he used the trick he'd learned the first morning and tossed the covers back.

While it wasn't freezing, the air was cool enough to shock her, and she rolled onto her back. Glaring at him, she muttered, "You need to stop doing that."

It took everything he had to keep his eyes on her face and not on her delectable naked body. "We have to be at the Protector building in about an hour. Unless you want to show up unwashed and smelling of me, you need to hop into the shower."

Stretching her arms overhead, she replied, "I'd only smell of you if I were pregnant, which I very much hope doesn't happen anytime soon."

He noted that she didn't say never, just not soon. His dragon stood up tall. *Good. One day, she will bear our young.*

Hush. There are more important things to focus on today.

Unable to completely resist Honoria's body, he danced his fingers against her side. She jerked and barked out a laugh at the same time. "Don't do that, Ash."

"Why not? You always say my fingers are warm."

She raised an eyebrow. "Because your fingers have a habit of wandering, and we don't have time for that. Especially since we have no idea what today's task or test will be. On top of that, you tend to forget things the hour after you orgasm, and that would be a disaster. So you're going to have to wait."

He leaned down and positioned his face just over hers. “Just for the time being?”

A wicked glint filled her eyes. “You’ll know when it’s time to bring out the hanky-panky again.”

The corner of his mouth ticked up. “You spent far too much time in America.”

She winked. “It just adds to my charm.”

It would be so easy to fall in love with Honoria again.

He stilled at that thought. No, he couldn’t risk loving her because it might also put the clan’s future in jeopardy. And for at least the next few years, the clan needed to be a top priority, until they were stable and somewhat cohesive again.

His beast growled, but Asher simply said, *Don’t.*

The tone was enough to keep his beast quiet, but Honoria’s voice filled the room. “Your face turned serious just then. What happened?”

Shaking his head, he sat upright again. “Not now. We need to save and focus all our energy for whatever will happen in about an hour.”

She searched his gaze. “We can’t be a team if you won’t talk to me.”

“After we complete whatever the DDA has planned, we can talk about it then.”

She rolled her eyes. “If that tone is supposed to make me submit, it’s not going to work.”

Asher turned and moved to the edge of the bed, until his feet touched the ground. “After, Ria. I promise I’ll talk more after.”

Not that he had any fucking clue what he’d say to her. If he spoke the truth about how he could see himself falling back in love with her and wanting a future together, it could complicate everything.

His beast whispered, *Or, it could finally slide everything into place.*

With a growl, Asher stood and walked toward the bathroom. "I'll shower first."

He risked one last glance at Honoria and nearly blinked at the stubbornness in her gaze, as well as the firmness of her jaw. He knew that look—she wouldn't stop until she found out the truth.

It seemed that he'd have to prepare for two things now, because the instant their next task was over, Honoria would pounce on him. And not in a hanky-panky way, either.

Once he reached the bathroom, he turned on the cold water in the shower. Stepping under the freezing spray, he closed his eyes. Part of him wanted her to find out the truth, and the remaining part wanted to run. Asher hadn't had a nightmare during the past week, but one was waiting to happen. And when it did, Honoria might see him as less of a male and/or a worthy partner.

And that was something he couldn't endure.

The rational thing would be to stop their dalliances and focus on the clan.

But that thought left a sour taste in his mouth.

His dragon finally spoke again. *Don't push her aside. She is meant to be ours, even if she's not our true mate.*

He didn't say anything to his beast, but mulled over the words for a few minutes before forcing his brain to focus on all the new facts and information he'd learned from Honoria over the last three days. He couldn't fuck up what came next, or he could risk everyone's future, not just his own.

~~~

Asher dodging Honoria's question and acting as if
~~~

everything was normal, and then her not doing anything about it, was bloody difficult. Over the last three days, she thought they'd fallen back into old times, which meant being comfortable around one another and holding less and less back from the other.

Sure, the sex had been fantastic, but discussing the recent history surrounding the dragon clans in England and Scotland, or even about their leaders, had been just as amazing. No one back in the US had really cared about the faraway English clan or their UK compatriots. In a way, it had been as if she'd lost a part of who she was when she'd left Skyhunter.

But now, she was back and about to tackle the next task with Asher at her side. She'd just have to focus on that and press Asher for details later.

Her dragon spoke up. *You worry too much. Besides, he may act normal, but he was a prisoner and supposedly tortured. It can't be easy for him.*

Shame flooded her body. *I think I do forget about that sometimes. But he never bloody talks about it. Asher should know that he can tell us anything.*

Right, because dragonmen are always open and honest about their feelings, her beast drawled.

Honoria smiled. *One can hope.*

Her dragon snorted as they rounded the last corner to the main security building. She glanced over at Asher and noticed his pupils flashing between slits and round. She had no idea what he was talking to his dragon about, but she was glad he was. One thing she'd learned about his imprisonment was how his dragon had been drugged silent for most of the five years they'd been locked up.

And for a lesser male, that could've led to insanity. But not Asher, the stubborn and wonderful dragonman he was.

Her dragon added, *And he's as dominant as we are. Don't forget that.*

You only appreciate that when we're naked. I'm sure it's going to drive you crazy later.

Her dragon huffed. *We'll see. All it'll take is some training to get him to do what I want, and I have loads of ideas.*

She bit her lip to keep from laughing. If she did, Asher would ask about it and then she'd have to explain her dragon's randy desires.

Asher caught her eye and raised his brows. "Are you ready?"

Banishing all humor from her countenance, she stood taller. "Of course I am. Are you?"

The corner of his mouth ticked up. "If we keep questioning each other, this isn't going to end well."

She shrugged. "It'll just take time to figure out how we work best together, that's all."

"I suppose."

Honoria yearned to reach over and take Asher's hand in reassurance, but they'd agreed to nix any public displays of affection and save it for private.

Her dragon muttered, *Stupid rule. Dragon-shifters don't hide affection. That's a human thing.*

For the time being, our every move is going to be watched by a few humans. So it's best to try and not surprise them too much.

Imagine if we reached over and squeezed Ash's arse. I bet the DDA human's mouth would drop open, or maybe she'd even faint.

Honoria couldn't help it, she laughed. When Asher sent her a questioning gaze, she shook her head. "Later."

His gaze lingered a second before he returned the nod. And for good reason—they'd arrived at the main security building for the clan.

They nodded at the young Protector manning the front door and walked inside. As they were guided to a room by another Protector, Honoria whispered, "I wonder if it's a group test or a team one."

Upon hearing of Honoria and Asher's arrangement, the remaining candidates had teamed up, too.

Asher replied, "We'll find out in about ten seconds, provided we're all gathered together. I rather hope not, though. I'd rather focus on showing our best assets during an individual trial."

The young Protector stopped next to a door and said, "This is as far as I go. They're waiting for you in there."

The "they" part of his sentence piqued her curiosity.

Asher opened the door and Honoria walked in. She promptly blinked at who sat behind a long table.

While she'd never met either of the dragon-shifters in person, the dark-haired, blue-eyed form of Bram Moore-Llewellyn and the blond-haired, brown-eyed form of Finlay Stewart were well known to her—and to most anyone in the UK, truth be told—from pictures and interviews.

It looked like the clan leaders of Stonefire and Lochguard had come to question them.

Bram spoke first and motioned toward the empty chairs opposite him. "Take a seat. I promise I won't bite, but I can't make any promises about Finn here."

Finn grinned. "If I'm going to bite, you won't see it coming."

Bram sighed. "I thought we talked about toning it down a fraction?"

"Aye, but I never agreed to it, if you remember."

Bram grunted. "Then why did you nod at the time?"

"Oh, that? Aye, well, I was remembering a tune I sang to my daughter. You just mistook it for agreement."

Bram let out an even bigger sigh, and muttered, "You promised Ara you'd behave."

The Stonefire leader referred to Finn's dragon-shifter mate, Arabella MacLeod. By all accounts, she was the center of Finn's world, along with his three children.

As Honoria slid into one of the seats, she couldn't help but smile. "What they say about you two is true, then."

Bram raised a dark eyebrow. "I'm almost afraid to ask what's true." He motioned toward the other leader and drawled, "Being connected to anything which involves Finn is asking for trouble."

A laugh escaped her lips before she could stop it. "That you two act more like brothers than anything else."

Bram shook his head as Finn winked. The blond Scottish leader spoke first. "Thank you, lass. You just made my day. Bram hates it when people say that, and anything that irritates him only improves my mood."

Honoria looked over at Asher, who sat quietly watching the pair. He finally jumped in. "I suspect this is an act to put us at ease before you pounce?"

Bram raised his brows. "I wish I could say yes, but this Scottish bastard is determined to ruin our images."

Finn waved a hand in dismissal. "If we're to maybe work with this pair in the future, they should know what they're getting into, aye?"

Honoria spoke up again. "So you're not against a co-leader team?"

Finn shook his head. "No. It's a clever idea, truth be told. Not that I'd want to share it with anyone, mind you. My family likes to meddle, and no doubt several of them would want to jump in and help. Which is all fine, until it turns into some kind of wee disaster."

Bram smirked. "And I'll make sure to mention that to your mate when I talk with her next. She is your family, too, after all."

Asher spoke before Finn could reply. "Then if you're not against a male-female team wanting to lead, then why are you here?"

Finn's eyes turned assessing, and Honoria nearly did a double-take at how quickly his carefree demeanor turned into one of shrewd intelligence. Finn said, "To judge your characters. Marcus King was a bastard who hurt a lot of people. Lochguard may be hundreds of miles north of here, but Marcus's actions affected us, too. And I'm not about to allow another arsehole to take over and possibly harm my clan again."

All eyes turned to Asher, and Honoria waited to see what he'd do. She suspected there was a motive behind everything, but she wasn't attuned enough yet to figure it out.

Which bloody irritated her, but all she could do was wait and see.

Some would be distracted by the Stonefire and Lochguard leaders' charm, but Asher wasn't going to fall for it. After all, at one time, his uncle had been charming. Until he hadn't been and instead had decided fear would work better to control the clan.

His dragon spoke up. *Given what we learned, I doubt these two will use fear.*

Maybe, maybe not. They haven't earned my trust yet.

Nor have we earned theirs.

I know, but I won't cower. Even if they're allies, dragon clans are still semiautonomous.

Once Finn answered about wanting to protect his clan, Asher leaned forward in his seat and said, "One meeting isn't going to accomplish much in terms of judging our characters."

Finn nodded. "Aye, you're right. Which is why we're staying for a wee while. And just know that me being here means I had to leave my mate and triplets behind. So tread carefully as my usually brilliant, hilarious self will be a little less forgiving at times, especially if it comes to displays of dominance."

At the steel in the Scottish dragonman's voice, Asher raised his brows. "If you think a mere threat will scare me enough to keep me in line, then you don't know a fucking thing about what happened here."

Honoria murmured his name, but he kept his gaze on Finn. The dragonman finally bobbed his head. "Aye, you're right. I don't know exactly what happened here since Skyhunter didn't share information with either of our clans for over a decade. But any male who'd bury dead bodies on his land and plotted with humans to take down other dragon-shifters can't have been a good leader."

Before he could reply, Honoria spoke up. "He wasn't. He killed my parents and threw Ash in prison for five years."

Bram glanced at him, Honoria, and back again. "Then is this some sort of revenge-based act?"

"No," Asher stated. "Skyhunter is my home. The clan needs good leadership if it's to survive and heal. It won't be easy, but I think Ria and I have the best chance of doing it."

Finn tilted his head. "Oh, aye? And why is that?"

Honoria answered, "Because I helped develop new types of technology we can use to bring the clan into the present. I perfected it and its implementation in America, and not even your clans have similar systems. And as for Ash, he has the knowledge of everyone inside Skyhunter and who would be the best fit for the various new roles going forward."

Under the table, Honoria took his hand and squeezed. The small gesture helped to ground him and make him focus on what was important, which wasn't prodding the two dragon-shifter leaders. "Not to mention we plan to divvy up specialized tasks, so that individuals can focus on specifics, rather than having one person try to tackle everything and stretch themselves too thin. As far as I know, none of the other candidates have the same idea."

Bram said, "Dividing up the tasks and handing off some responsibility would definitely make our mates happy."

"Aye," Finn stated. "And the bairns. It's definitely something to think about for the future. Lorcan is due to step down soon, and his successor might be open to the idea, too."

Asher knew Lorcan Todd was the older leader of Northcastle, the dragon-shifter clan in Northern Ireland. But he didn't remember too much beyond that.

Bram studied Asher a second before saying, "You two seem to be coordinated in some way already, answering when the other pauses, and even comforting when needed—aye, I noticed that, too. So tell me, are you two true mates?"

Asher had never thought he'd want a mate, but for the first time, he wished fate had made Honoria his true mate.

His dragon huffed. *Fate doesn't matter. Share everything and she can be ours.*

Honoria squeezed his fingers tighter and answered, "No. Although we did date as teenagers. And whilst we've each changed a bit since then, it definitely helps us understand one another most of the time. Although occasionally, he gets all alpha dragonman-like and I don't understand a bloody thing."

The leaders chuckled, but Asher couldn't tear his gaze from Honoria. She would always be able to make him smile, and with enough time, could probably chase away most of the darkness from his prison stint.

If not for everything that could end up on their shoulders, Asher would pull Honoria close, kiss her, and say she should be his mate.

However, duty was a priority, so he refrained. True, he should let go of her hand, too, but he couldn't bring himself to do it.

Bram's voice garnered Asher's attention again. "I'll admit we all act that way from time to time, and I doubt our mates will ever understand us completely." He paused and in the blink of an eye, the laughter vanished from Bram's face. "And whilst I don't care if you two shag each other when the mood strikes, we need to know if it'll affect your ability to lead, especially if either of you turns to someone else later in life."

His beast growled. *I don't want anyone else, just Ria.*

Honoria replied, "It won't. Both of us love this clan and want to see it return to what it once was. After all, when we were small children, Skyhunter was one of the most open and understanding clans in the UK."

Finn jumped in. "I think we're all fairly close in age, which means I don't remember anything from before the age of nine or so and can't remember that version of Skyhunter. I'll just have to take your word for it."

Bram tapped his hand on the table a few times. "Well, so far, you seem fairly arsehole-free. But we'll see how things go over the next week or so."

Asher frowned. "Exactly how long are you going to be on Skyhunter?"

The Stonefire leader shrugged. "As long as is necessary." Finn opened his mouth, but Bram continued, "And we both have to agree when it's time to leave. I'm as anxious to get back to my family as you are, Finn, but if we want a good future for our children, this is important, too."

"Considering your mate is pregnant right now, that's very magnanimous of you, Bram," Finn stated.

Not wanting to think of pregnant mates—because then he'd start imagining what it'd be like to have a family of his own, something Asher had doubted he'd ever have since his imprisonment—he released Honoria's hand and stood. "Right, then I think we're done for now."

Bram remained seated. "Aye, for the moment. However, we'll be popping up at random times, to see how things are going."

Finn winked. "But don't worry, we'll make sure to knock first, aye?"

Asher didn't know the males well enough to joke about sex, especially with Honoria at his side, so he turned halfway toward the door. "Until later, then."

Once both the leaders nodded in parting, Asher turned and exited the room. Honoria murmured something he couldn't hear before joining him. However, as he made the turn toward the building's exit, the human Penny appeared from out of a room and blocked their path. "Er, no, you're not quite done yet. Once all the interviews are finished, there's another test today. Well, two, really. The first is a quick test on a tablet whilst you wait for the others. This way."

Asher held his tongue and followed the human into the room. He hoped the second test was something physical, as he needed it. Both he and his dragon liked to spend some time outside in the mornings, as a reminder that they were free and wouldn't be going back to a small, dark cell.

His beast spoke up. *It's okay. Maybe we should take Ria for a flight instead of rushing her to bed again.*

That isn't something I thought you'd ever say.

I want to know everything about her, as do you. If it means one day she becomes our mate, I can wait a while for more sex.

Asher was careful to keep a neutral expression on his face. *You keep talking of mates. But what of the clan?*

We can have both.

You don't know that.

Yes, I do. Ria will make us stronger.

A tablet was thrust into his hands, and Asher did his best to ignore his dragon and take the test.

He could feel Honoria staring at him, but she wouldn't cause a stir in public. However, they would be having more than a few words later, that he was certain of.

But for the moment, Asher responded to the strange situational questions. A clan leader needed to focus at will, and Asher was more than up to prove he could.

Chapter Seven

Honoria could tell from Asher's clenched jaw that something was on his mind.

The talk—or had it been an interview?—with Bram and Finn had been somewhat strange. But she didn't think Asher was worrying about the two leaders. She watched him closer than she probably should and had noticed the change when asked about being true mates.

Her dragon spoke up. *I bet his dragon thinks like me—that we'd be a good fit.*

I thought you said they needed more training?

Her beast sniffed. *They do, but they're still far better than any other male we've met.*

She should drop it. After all, there was another trial coming up and she should be psyching herself up for it.

But she replied before she could talk herself out of it. *But is it truly a good idea? I mean, things could easily go wrong.*

I have faith. Why don't you?

She stole a glance at Asher. She was coming to love everything about him, from the scar on his face representing how strong he was, to how he wasn't afraid to take comfort from her touch, to even his ability to stand up to other clan leaders no matter how famous they were. And all of that was still only the tip of the iceberg of what made up Asher King.

Truthfully, she was halfway in love with him again. She replied, *Maybe. Let's see if we can win this thing first, and then worry about our personal lives.*

So you're open to it then?

I suppose so. But it takes two people in a relationship, and if Asher doesn't learn to open up to us, it may be doomed before it even starts.

He'll tell us when he's ready. Just be patient.

Says the dragon-shifter who demanded sex ad nauseam until she got it.

That improved all of our chances of winning. There was a purpose behind it.

Honoria doubted that was her dragon's main reason for the badgering, but she focused back on the tablet in her hands and went through the questions. Each was a situation that could come up for a clan—such as trade negotiations with the local counties, or dealing with enemies such as the dragon hunters or Dragon Knights—and she answered as best she could. The other candidates came in sporadically, but she did her best to ignore them.

Only when she finished the last question did she survey the others taking the same test on their tablets. While she wasn't familiar with all the people beyond the public information she'd found, there was one glaringly obvious difference—she was the only female in the room. It seemed there were only two other sets competing along with her and Asher. Although how Shane Farhall had made it this far, she had no idea.

Her beast spoke up. *He probably learned things from his older brother, even if Shane was in Wales and his brother here.*

Shane's older brother had been head Protector under the old leader. *I'm not sure how that's a positive.*

It probably means he knows how to give good-sounding answers.

That won't be enough for Bram and Finn.

For all we know, they could be keeping him in to push the rest of us.

Yes, that sounds more reasonable. Or, so Honoria hoped. Shane's temper should've gotten him disqualified already.

While she waited for everyone else to complete the task, Honoria did her best to memorize the faces and any sort of ticks and tells she noticed on the other contestants. The smallest detail could be the deciding factor in who won the trials.

Eventually, the final male-male pair raised their tablets and handed them over to the DDA human. Once Penny put them aside, she clapped her hands. "Right, then it's time to do the next section. This bit will be more familiar to you, as it involves physical tests that push your mind to the brink." She looked at each pair in turn. "And since all of you are competing as teams, there is one important difference. Both of you must complete the set of tasks and remain together at all times. If you leave your teammate behind—well, beyond short distances as laid out in the materials you'll receive—you'll be disqualified."

One of the males spoke up. "What if our teammate is injured? Should we leave them to find help?"

"Of course, but that still will disqualify you. You see, this is a true test under pressure. You will be going in blind, with only three rules. The first is you're not allowed to kill or mortally wound anyone. The second is you must remain within the confines of South Downs National Park. Where the park runs along the Channel, you may fly up to fifty feet within shore. But otherwise, you must remain in the park. And lastly, even though it should go without saying, you can't interact with or disrupt the humans in the area. We have eyes, ears, and CCTV cameras everywhere, so don't think you can cheat and get away with it." Penny motioned toward the door. "If you agree to these rules and wish to carry on, you need to gather in pairs at the main landing area. Robin will give you the first set of instructions before releasing you in timed intervals."

It looked as if the trials would finally be heating up and becoming competitive.

Her dragon grunted. *Good. All of these human things are boring. I'm ready to fly and explore.*

We don't even know what the task will be.

No, but if one of the rules is to stay within South Downs, then it involves leaving the clan.

Honoria didn't hesitate to stand, nor did Asher, and they exited the building. Her dragon shuffled her feet impatiently inside her mind, anxious to get started. She said to her beast, *Just wait. If we rush, we could miss something.*

Her dragon fell silent, and once they were outside, she whispered for Asher's ears only, "From here on out, communication is key. We *must* work together and share everything, lest we be disqualified."

Asher nodded, a smile curving his lips. "I like it when you're bossy." She narrowed her eyes and he grinned. "Okay, okay, I get it—no teasing right now." His expression turned serious. "And yes, share everything and stick together, no matter how difficult things become."

She wanted to take his hand, but resisted. Now wasn't the time.

Her dragon spoke up. *Why not? It may make the others underestimate us. After all, they'll think we're a scared female, looking for comfort from her male to protect her.*

She mentally snorted. *True.*

Reaching over, she took Asher's hand. His gaze found hers, but she gave an infinitesimal shake of her head. Asher must've understood because he looked straight ahead once more.

A quick glance over her shoulder revealed Shane pointing toward them.

Her dragon spoke up. *See? I told you.*

Yes, so keep your ideas coming. I may not agree with all of them, but we need to work together as best we can, too.

So in reality, it's the four of us who make up the team—two humans and two dragons.

Two bloody good humans and dragons. The landing area came into view. *So let's do this.*

As they made their way toward the tall form of Robin, Honoria kept her head high and shoulders back. The next set of tasks could determine everything, and she was more than ready to get started.

Asher suspected Honoria had reached for his hand to put on a show and make Shane, and maybe some of the others, think she was afraid. It was brilliant, but it also irked him a little. He didn't like others thinking Honoria weak, even if it was part of a plan.

His dragon spoke up. *Give it time. People are still trying to wrap their heads around the female leader in Ireland, and it's been months since her secret was revealed. Honoria throwing her name into the race and it going public was only days ago.*

It was hard to think it'd been barely a week since he'd first spotted the blonde hair and blue eyes of Honoria in the conference room.

Robin's tall, dark-skinned form came into view and Asher quickly packed away his irritation. They were about to learn their first task.

Once they reached the Protector, he handed them a satchel used for when in dragon form, meaning it could easily be clutched in the hind legs or around a dragon's neck. Robin motioned toward the bag. "Inside you'll find your assignment and supplies. I can't say more than that, so don't ask. You have five minutes to read and study your material before you must depart. Good luck."

Robin walked away to the side of the main landing area to guard two other large satchels.

Not wasting a minute, Asher opened it and found a small envelope with the words "READ FIRST" emblazoned on the front, a basic first-aid kit, one hundred pounds, a binder full of the necessary intel from the Protectors, and a square device with a single button encased in a clear plastic cover. On the back of the button device were the words, "Press only for emergencies. Disqualified once pressed."

Honoria placed it back in the bag. "We won't be using that then." She picked up the envelope. Inside was a note as well as a picture of a ginger-haired male in his late twenties, the intricate tattoo on his bicep marking him a dragon-shifter. He had no bloody clue who the male was.

Asher took the note and read it aloud, "Fraser MacKenzie has been kidnapped by the dragon hunters and is trapped somewhere in South Downs. Your goal is to find him, carefully extract him, and return him to Skyhunter, where he can be reunited with his clan leader, Finlay Stewart."

Honoria spoke up. "So it seems the clan cooperation continues."

Asher studied the male's features, including the amusement in his eyes and the shadow of a smile on his lips. "And knowing my luck, he'll be a pain in my arse to get back."

Honoria chuckled. "That's part of the challenge." She stashed the note and picture back inside the satchel. "We should go. How about going to our special spot first, to go through all the information in the binder and strategize?"

He loved how Honoria went straight to the point, and he grunted. "We'll probably need our clothes at some point, so let's toss them into the bag, too."

Once they undressed and did so, Asher took a second to watch Honoria's form change. White wings grew from her back, her arms and legs extended, and her face morphed into a dragon's snout and ears. The urge to chase her in the skies rushed through his body.

When she stood in her beautiful white dragon form, he met her gaze and read her look, which told him to hurry his arse up.

His dragon laughed as they shifted. And when done, he tossed the satchel around his neck, spread his red wings, crouched down, and jumped into the air. After a few beats of his wings, he was high enough to find his bearings and head toward his and Honoria's special place.

It'd been more than a decade since he'd visited it. However, both male and dragon knew exactly where it was, nestled not far from Arundel Castle but beyond the Duke of Norfolk's lands.

When he spotted a particular old stone bridge on the River Arun, Asher adjusted his wings and headed for a tree-covered hill that overlooked the river.

He carefully landed onto the small clearing at the top of it and imagined his body shrinking back into his human form. Once he and Honoria were both done, Asher didn't waste time taking out the binder compiled by the Protectors.

Honoria leaned against his side as he opened it. He was aware of every inch of her skin pressed against his, almost as if the heat of her body was transferring to his. Not to mention the spark continued on down to his cock, which was already stirring to life.

It made it fucking impossible to concentrate on the task at hand.

His dragon spoke up. *You could tell her to move.*

Never.

Clan leaders should be able to resist even the most delectable female at his side. Drawing on his years of experience in prison, when he had perfected the art of distraction, Asher remembered the ginger-haired male who was their target. He was the key to winning Skyhunter. Only then could he claim Honoria as his, maybe forever.

And so he scanned the documents inside the binder.

There were several suspected locations listed of where the dragon hunters could be hiding. On top of that, there were several fuzzy photographs included, each with a label of when and where they'd been spotted.

Honoria whispered, "I think we should identify the most important and reliable information and start narrowing down the possible locations." He glanced at her and she raised her brows. "What? It's not as if we're going to close our eyes, place a finger on the list, and pick one that way."

The corner of his mouth ticked up. "Of course not. But I was thinking exactly the same thing."

She winked. "Great minds think alike."

Once their assignment was done, Asher would most definitely bring Honoria back here and make this spot theirs in more ways than one.

His dragon snorted. *Now who's the randy one? Stop thinking with our dick and focus.*

He gave Honoria a quick kiss and motioned toward the list. "I think we should cross off any that rely on secondary and tertiary information and stick with the primary accounts."

Honoria nodded. "I agree. The further away from the original source, the more likely the information gets distorted. Even if some of the suspected locations are closer to Skyhunter and our current position, we can always check them, if need be, as we make our way back home."

"Right, and so it might be worthwhile to fly to the farthest site and work our way backward. Then we don't lose track of where we've been or have to waste time backtracking."

Honoria's long, elegant finger ran down the list. The sight motivated him—the sooner they finished the blasted test, the sooner her fingers could run along his skin.

She tapped a finger at one of the locations toward the bottom. "How about we start here. It's at the western edge of South Downs."

He nodded. "Right, but let's land far enough away so no one will see us in the sky and raise an alarm. Whilst it'll take longer, approaching the last few miles by foot means we can take care of any sentries and look for the secret entrances mentioned."

"But we need to stay clear of the village near it, too. So we should probably land just to the south of the location."

Asher closed the binder and put it into the satchel. "Right, let's go."

He tried to take a step away, but Honoria grabbed his bicep and kissed him gently on the lips. "For luck."

While not one to believe in luck, he kissed her back and nodded. "No more delays. I'm sure whoever completes the task in the shortest amount of time will win."

Honoria raced to the other side of the clearing. "Then try to keep up with me."

Her body morphed into her white dragon form, and she jumped into the sky.

Asher scrambled to shift and follow her. Female dragons were smaller physically, but they were bloody fast.

His dragon laughed. *It's good because we like to chase her.*

Not disagreeing with his beast, Asher picked up his speed and headed toward their first destination.

Chapter Eight

After two days with almost no food or sleep, Honoria lightly smacked her cheeks to wake herself up.

Asher's whisper came from in front of her. "Do you need a break?"

"No, no, I'll be fine for another hour."

Glancing over his shoulder, he raised his brows in concern. "Are you sure?"

Some might think Asher was being overprotective. And while he no doubt was—the trait was pretty much hardwired into male dragon-shifter DNA—he was also thinking of their task. If they didn't take enough breaks, they could miss the smallest detail, one that could lead them to find the right place and complete the bloody challenge.

She bobbed her head. "Yes, I'm sure. Besides, we should be close to the third location on our list. We can rest after, if this place isn't the right one."

He nodded and faced forward again, picking their way through the underbrush. Honoria did her best to keep her eyes and ears peeled in the predawn light. Even with her enhanced sight and sound, all thanks to her dragon-shifter genes, it took time and concentration to separate sounds from one another in the woods, let alone try to identify them.

Her dragon spoke up. *I won't miss anything. Save your strength for investigating the site, just in case it's the correct one.*

She smiled. *Thanks, but no. We need to work together on this. Especially since we have no idea if someone had a better approach to their task and already found their captive.*

Her beast huffed. *There's no way Shane and his partner would beat us. He's all bluster, no brains.*

Cockiness will end in failure, dragon. Besides, I doubt the Stonefire and Lochguard leaders would make this easy. After all, they've both had to deal with the bastard hunters and Knights more than a few times. It might be more realistic than we expect, meaning it could be a bloody fine line between saving the captive and getting him killed.

Just remembering stories of how one of Stonefire's Protectors—a female named Charlie—had been drained to death of her blood by the dragon hunters made Honoria shiver. She added, *Skyhunter might've had Marcus, but each clan has had their own trials and tragedies, too.*

Which is why it's important to work together. I think—

Her beast paused at the same time she and Asher did, at the sound of whispers. She couldn't make out the murmured words, but she could definitely detect at least two humans or dragon-shifter voices nearby.

Asher turned and stood closer to her side. They both listened, but the voices vanished in an instant.

Either they had stopped talking midsentence, or they'd disappeared into a soundproofed structure or even an underground tunnel of some sort.

Her dragon said, *I think tunnel. There wasn't any sort of hesitation in their speech cadence.*

Normally, I would tease you about trying to be an expert in voices, but I think you're right. However, they still could be inside a building.

There would be some kind of scent—of wood, paint, building materials. But there's none of that. I think it's a tunnel.

Taking a second, Honoria tried to find any scent that was out of place in a forest. And beyond a small whiff of plastic, her dragon was correct. Nothing suggested a building nearby.

Her beast stood taller inside her mind. *Of course I'm right. I told you I'm good at this.*

Honoria leaned over to Asher's ear and whispered as low as she could, "We should circle around, ensure no one else is standing watch, and find out where they went. I think it's a tunnel."

Moving his lips her ear, he answered, "I agree. I'll take the right side, you the left. We'll meet back here when done. If no one's about, we can look for a hidden entrance."

With a nod, she went to the left. Honoria's fatigue had vanished thanks to the adrenaline currently pumping through her veins, and she had no trouble scanning the surroundings and listening for anything unusual. While some might be grateful for the growing daylight, she wasn't. The sooner they could find the entrance—she was certain there was one—the sooner they could vanish from the woods and tackle the next phase.

Asher surveyed his half of the area and was almost disappointed when he didn't find anyone.

His dragon spoke up. *Things can't be exciting all the time.*

I know, but it'd be nice to do more than track down someone and bring them back. A little exertion would wake us up a bit more anyway. And no, not that *kind of exertion. No sex until this is done.*

His beast sniffed. *I wasn't going to suggest it. I thought you might like to know I saw a tiny flashing light a second ago. But maybe you're not interested.*

Asher stilled. *Where was it?*

Thankfully his dragon didn't hold back or give him a hard time. *Five steps backward, and then look toward the northwest.*

He backtracked and looked in the correct direction. And there, he saw it. A small flashing white light. *You think they would've remembered to shade that.*

Or, it could be part of the trial and is a trick.

Perhaps. But let's quickly survey the last little bit of our half and then find Honoria.

Asher moved as fast as he could, careful to make as little noise as possible. Neither he nor his dragon spotted anything else unusual, which meant the flashing light was probably where the two voices had disappeared to.

At their original starting point, he saw Honoria already waiting. He sometimes forgot how silently fast she could be.

Once he was close enough he could almost press his lips to her ear, he whispered, "I found a blinking light that might be an entrance. Did you see anything unusual on your half?" She shook her head and he continued, "Then we should go investigate. Are you ready? Or, should we rest first?"

She moved her head so she could reply to his ear, "Clan leaders don't get to wait for a convenient time. Besides, it'll be easier to sneak about whilst it's mostly dark outside. Let's go."

Of course, she was right. Anyone who thought Honoria was too weak or emotional to be a clan leader because she was a female clearly didn't know her at all.

His dragon grunted. *We can extol her virtues later. If we keep standing around here, who knows, Shane might end up beating us.*

Fuck if I'll let that happen.

He and Honoria quickly discussed their plan, and Asher guided her to where the white light flashed slowly in the predawn light. Funny to think that if they'd done this an hour later, they might've missed it because of the sunshine. Yet another thing he needed to thank Honoria for—pushing them both to keep going. He would have to remember to do that for her in the future, too. She was strong, but there would be times she'd need his strength as well.

They stood just to the side of the blinking light, and Asher waited for Honoria to use the technical knowledge she'd amassed in America as part of her training to determine if it was an alarm or not. And if so, whether it could be disarmed or not.

After a few seconds, she plucked the blinking light off and tossed it to the side. She whispered, "A decoy alarm. It's just a flashing light poking out of a plastic box."

"That doesn't mean there's nothing."

"Right, so prepare yourself for what could be inside."

She moved to look for a door, but he pushed her to the side and did it himself. No doubt she'd yell at him later, but if it was a trap and it triggered some sort of gun or explosion, he couldn't watch as Honoria got hurt.

His dragon huffed. *She might not see it as chivalrous.*

Too bad.

Asher finally found a hidden latch, looked at Honoria, and nodded.

Taking a deep breath, he tugged lightly. A door swung outward, and nothing else happened beyond revealing a dimly lit corridor.

He pointed to his chest, raised one finger, and then pointed to the hallway. Honoria nodded, raised two fingers and pointed to her own chest, meaning yes, he could go first, thank fuck. Just the thought of something happening to her made his stomach churn.

His beast spoke up. *Stop worrying about her until it's necessary. Otherwise, this partnership will never work.*

Hush and focus on the task at hand.

While there was no guarantee this was even the right spot, Asher's gut said it was.

Which meant any misstep could disqualify them, such as if they were caught by some mysterious guards. He would need to trust Honoria.

Asher moved down the hallway, Honoria close on his heels. Beyond the compacted dirt floor and the occasionally flickering lights, he didn't hear or see anything else. Due to the aged lighting and spots of corroded metal on the wall supports, he could tell the tunnel wasn't new, though. It was probably a relic from the Second World War.

The corridor curved slightly before going down a set of steep metal stairs. They were slick with condensation, so he took each one carefully, not wanting to slip.

They both reached the bottom, only to find another door. Asher eased it open. The instant he did, a series of cries came from the other side.

"Food, please, give me some food. I haven't eaten in days. Tell me you're bringing me some food."

"Where's my mummy? I want my mummy." Sniffle. "Where's my mummy?"

"You bastards will pay when my clan leader back in Ireland hears about this."

And the various pleadings and threats only amplified, until he could barely make them out from one another.

Asher poked his head in and saw a series of cells, the voices belonging to each of the prisoners. Some were men, others teenagers, and one even contained a young child.

A flashback to when Asher had been half-dragged back to his cell, past the ones used for children and teenagers, came back to him. All of them had begged for help, food, water, and their parents. They had also pleaded that if he escaped, to get them out.

At the time, Asher had found just enough energy to knock out one guard and then the other. But just as he went to open the cell and let the kids out, someone had shot him with a tranquilizer dart. His vision had faded, a mixture of crying children and something he suspected was his own blood were the last things he'd seen.

Waking up hadn't been pretty, either. His cousin had made sure Asher knew he'd broken the rules. Even though his arm had healed within days, it hadn't hurt any less when it had been snapped in two.

Honoria's voice drifted through his nightmarish flashback. "Asher, are you with me? Asher."

His dragon also spoke up. *I'm here, too. You're not* there*, when I couldn't reach you.*

Shaking his head to clear it, he glanced quickly at Honoria. "Sorry. I'll be fine now."

Curiosity burned in her blue-eyed gaze, but she merely nodded and whispered, "Then let's keep going. Maybe one of them is the male we're looking for."

"Be careful. This could still be a trap."

As they walked and checked each of the cells, Asher did his best to focus on his assignment and not the prisoners. They all looked clean, well-fed, and not the least bit tortured, like what he'd seen during his five-year-long imprisonment.

All of the prisoners crying out and acting were probably part of their task. If they discovered not, then he'd find a way to free them. But first things first, they needed to search for the red-haired male from the photo. The instructions required them to find and rescue him first, before they tried to help anyone else. Otherwise, they'd be disqualified.

The hard part would be keeping his memories at bay. For all he knew, this set of cells was only the beginning.

His beast spoke up. *You have me and Ria. We'll help.*

At his dragon's words, Asher's small panic faded. Because even if he saw something else that triggered a flashback, Honoria would undoubtedly bring him back. As long as she was with him, he would find a way to carry on.

And so he did.

~~~

Honoria wanted to take Asher's hand as they went down the row of prison cells for both comfort and a reminder that he was here and not back in the past.

However, she might need both of her hands in a split second. So, she merely followed close behind him, doing her best to scan the cells and not let any of the pleading prisoners distract her.

Of course, that was easier said than done. The young children and teenagers were the hardest to ignore. Even if they were only playing a part, they probably shouldn't be underground in such a damp environment.

Her dragon spoke up. *I'm sure everything is closely monitored, if this is indeed all for the trial.*

It had better be, both for the monitoring and for this to be a task. Otherwise, we have no way of contacting the clan if this is a real hideout.

We do, as a last resort.

The emergency button sat heavy in her trouser pocket. *If it comes between a choice of saving these people or*
~~~

winning some task, I'll save these people in an instant.

And give up?

No bloody way. The others back home will get a persuasive earful. Because if the Stonefire and Lochguard leaders think following the rules to the letter is more important than saving lives, then they aren't the males I thought they were.

They reached another door, and Asher paused, glancing at her and raising his brows in question. She shook her head, letting him know she hadn't spotted the ginger-haired male from the photo yet.

He shook his head once, saying the same. So she motioned with her chin toward the door.

Asher gently pried it open, but unlike before, no sounds emerged. That could be good news, but it could also be quite bad.

For all they knew, the first corridor contained the healthier inmates, meaning the sick and injured could lay ahead.

Her dragon said softly, *Even if that's what happens, we can manage.*

I hope so. Blood and injuries have never been my thing, hence me studying business and technology.

When Asher moved, Honoria and her dragon stopped talking to focus on every scent, sound, and sight for the tiniest clue of what could lay ahead.

However, the same damp smell didn't tell her much, nor did the near-silence. Only the hum of old lighting and a distant fan for ventilation drifted to her ears, which wasn't overly helpful.

The oval-shaped room was empty, save for a few broken chairs and other rubbish that was probably older than she was.

After a thorough investigation to ensure there weren't

any secret latches or doorways, she and Asher approached yet another door.

With each one passed, they probably went deeper into the earth. Taking a long, even breath, Honoria pushed aside her bubbling panic. Dragon-shifters weren't meant to be underground.

And in that instant, she truly understood what hell it must've been for Asher to be underground for five long years.

Her beast grunted. *We can't change the past. It made him stronger. Nothing else matters.*

Asher struggled with the larger, heavier door. Honoria took one half of the handle and together they managed to heave it open, revealing a teenage girl tied to a chair, her head slumped to her chest.

She was alone, and Honoria did the quickest scan of their surroundings possible before rushing to the girl's side. She was breathing, and when Honoria touched her cheek, the young female stirred.

Her green eyes widened, and she struggled against her bindings. She pleaded, her accent marking her as Welsh, "Please, you have to get me out of here. They have my parents. And if I don't go after them, it could be too late. Please, they'll murder them, I know it."

The girl was like a younger version of Honoria. Except in her own case, she had been sent away to safety and had been unable to help her mum and dad when they'd needed it.

But with this girl, maybe she could act and save them, to try to make up for not doing anything for her own family.

Honoria reached for the bindings, but Asher grabbed her wrist. He whispered, "No. We can't."

The girl sniffled and started blubbering on about parents and something unintelligible.

Honoria didn't—no, couldn't—leave her here.

Asher's grip tightened at the same time as her dragon spoke up. *I know you want to, but we can't. If we do, without ensuring our target isn't here, we could be penalized.*

So now you care more about winning?

It's not that, and you know it.

As she watched the girl's tears and weaker struggles, Honoria's heart squeezed. Could she really just leave the girl here and keep going?

Asher's voice was barely a whisper at her ear. "I'm almost positive this is a set-up. First, bombarding me with the prison cells, and now a girl who is afraid her parents will be murdered? They're testing us, Ria. We can't let them win."

Asher's words cut through her desperation to save the girl. Having something from both their pasts, one right after the other, was too much of a coincidence.

One she never would've realized, though, if not for Asher pointing it out. Even now, the young female looked at her with big eyes, wanting her to help.

Taking a deep breath, she stood upright and backed away from the teenager. Even as the young female continued to struggle and sob, Honoria turned toward yet another blasted door. She murmured, "Come on."

With each step she took toward the door, Honoria only hoped she'd made the right decision.

Her beast chimed in, *If this is truly a dragon hunter or Dragon Knight den, then we'll find a way to save everyone. But what Asher said makes sense. It wouldn't surprise me if each of the candidates was being confronted with difficult aspects of their pasts and/or their fears, especially since each of us was researched thoroughly by the DDA. It's the perfect way to test how a dragon-shifter performs under pressure.*

Maybe, but sometimes coincidences happen. I won't rule out these people are truly prisoners until I spot Fraser MacKenzie.

Fair enough. Let's keep going and see if he's here.

It took both her and Asher to open the slightly smaller, but jammed door. Bracing herself for another dismal scene, she blinked when she saw the red-haired male sitting in a chair, his arms over his chest, whistling. "About bloody time," he stated in a Scottish accent.

They'd found their mark—Fraser MacKenzie.

Asher was glad he'd figured out what was going on, and even more so when Honoria believed him.

Between her being there for him in the row of cells, and he having her back with the struggling, sobbing teenager, it only reinforced how well they not only worked together but also how they balanced each other out.

His dragon spoke up. *Which means even if we have a nightmare, Honoria will be there to soothe us, just like today.*

Not wanting to have any sort of serious discussion about him and Honoria, he focused on opening yet another fucking door.

Of course, having the Scotsman whistle and complain about them finally arriving irritated him a fraction. He'd like to see the bastard go through hell over three days with little sleep and see how well he'd like someone being flippant.

His beast grunted. *Don't let him irritate you. Our job is to get him out and back to Skyhunter.*

Honoria spoke first. "Maybe we should leave and come back later, to let you enjoy this underground scenery a while longer."

Fraser snorted. “A lass with fire. If I weren’t happily mated already, I’d say I like it and might try to convince you to stay with me.”

The Scot winked, and Asher couldn’t prevent his growl. “This is no time for flirting. Will you come willingly, or do I need to knock your arse out and sling you over my shoulder?’

The male raised an eyebrow. “I may not be a Protector, but if I had to learn to keep up with my sister, I can certainly handle you.”

Honoria jumped in. “We’ll give you ten seconds to walk over to us and come willingly. If you don’t, then we’ll complete the task no matter what it takes.”

Shrugging, Fraser settled more into his chair. “The quiet was irritating at first, but I’m getting used to it. A wee while longer won’t kill me.”

He shared a glance with Honoria. Once she darted her eyes over to Fraser and back and winked, he understood. The dragonman would expect Asher to be the one to haul him out, not Honoria. All Asher had to do was distract the blasted male.

His beast spoke up. *I don’t know about that. His sister is Faye MacKenzie, right? She’s cohead Protector of Lochguard, which means he probably doesn’t dismiss females like most males do.*

Ria’s not going to walk straight up to him and punch the bastard in the face. I trust her to have a plan.

His beast fell silent in agreement, which he rather liked.

Asher faced Fraser and put his hands on his hips. “If you’re going to act like a child, then I’ll treat you like one. Let me count to ten slowly, and if you don’t get your sorry arse over here, then we’ll get you out one way or the other.”

Fraser snorted. “I’m the victim. You’re supposed to be nice to me, aye?”

Asher shrugged. "What if you were brainwashed by the hunters into believing you should stay? Being nice isn't always the best policy. Now, let's start the countdown. Ten....nine...eight..."

As he continued, Honoria moved a hand behind her back. From the corner of his eye, he saw her extend her talons. Even though he wanted to smile, he kept his attention on Fraser and continued counting down in an exasperated tone.

He reached one, and Fraser remained seated.

Honoria rushed forward, her talons at Fraser's cock and bollocks. She must've pressed against them because Fraser yelped. The Scottish dragon-shifter swore and demanded, "What the bloody hell are you doing?"

Honoria must've applied even more pressure because Fraser's forehead gleamed with a faint sheen of sweat. She shrugged one shoulder. "I thought you said you had a sister?"

"Aye, I do, but putting anyone's talons against another's genitals was against the rules."

She leaned forward, her tone intense. "In the real world, there aren't always rules."

His beast piped up. *She's fantastic.*

I agree.

Clearing his throat, Asher took a step toward the pair. "We can't mortally wound anyone, but I'm sure Ria could have a little fun without doing any serious harm. Should I leave her alone with you to do more convincing, or are you going to come with us willingly?"

"As if I have a fucking choice," Fraser muttered.

Honoria snorted. "You do, although most males are attached to certain parts of their bodies. To keep them intact, I think you'll come with us."

Fraser waved his hand, signaling for Honoria to move her talons. "I'll go as soon as you release me, bloody woman." Honoria did, and Fraser grunted. "Help choose the next leader, Finn said. It'll be fun, and you get to irritate them as much as you want, he said. Aye, well, this is the last time I listen to my sweet-talking cousin for quite some time."

As soon as Fraser stood, Asher glanced at Honoria. He asked, "Do you want the front or back?"

"Oh, I'll take the back. Easy access to poke between his thighs, in case I need to remind him to behave."

Asher did grin at both her words and the deep scowl on Fraser's face. "Sounds good to me. Now, come on. Who knows if there'll be anything to test us on the way out." Fraser opened his mouth, but Asher beat him to it. "And no, I'm not going to listen to you. Just be quiet, and I may try to stop Ria from making you a eunuch."

Fraser sighed, but Asher ignored him to nod at Honoria, letting her know he trusted her to watch his back. Then he went to the door and slowly opened it. However, the teenage girl from before was gone.

Not only that, but once they reached the row of jail cells, those were all empty, too.

Whoever had been in charge of this fake hideout was organized, to say the least.

He'd been just about to open the penultimate door, the one which leads to the stairs that would take them aboveground, when a boom reverberated through the room. Asher put a halt sign up with his hand and pressed his ear to the door. While it may have been thick enough to keep sound out for human ears, he detected a few voices on the other side but no footsteps on the metal stairs.

At least, not yet.

Glancing at Fraser, he whispered, "Try to escape, and

I'll do whatever it takes to subdue you."

Fraser shook his head. "There shouldn't be any other obstacles for this location. Well, unless..."

Honoria prodded, "Unless what? Time is of the essence."

Fraser glanced at Asher, to Honoria, and back again. "All three teams had the same information, leading them to this place. However, there are three staircases leading to three different scenarios. Depending on who approached the entrance, hidden panels would've shifted to lead each pair to the correct one. None of the others should be able to go down your designated staircase."

Asher cursed. "Which means one of the other teams could be breaking the rules, doing who the hell knows what to get the prize. If they threatened any of the others taking part, then it's possible they were shown how to reach the different staircases." He motioned toward the back of the row of cells. "There's a small space toward the back where they won't be able to see us from this entrance. Hurry, let's go there and form a plan."

Thankfully, Fraser didn't complain, and they all rushed to the small blind spot at the rear of the room. Fraser was pressed up against the wall behind them, with he and Honoria in front, giving them the chance to spring out and attack if needed.

Moving his head to Honoria's ear, he whispered, "Do you have a plan?"

"Actually, I do."

He listened and thought it was brilliant. Now all they had to do was wait.

Chapter Nine

As Honoria waited for whoever was coming, she did her best to breathe and stay at the ready.

She didn't know if her plan would work or not, but she was certain that at least one other pair had skirted the edge of the rules.

While none of them were allowed to kill or mortally wound, and they could only rescue one person for their task, there was nothing about coercing others for information. She only hoped it wasn't one of the younger participants.

Because if so, the sort of dragonman who would hurt anyone through interrogation—but especially children given how much dragon-shifters treasured them—should never be clan leader.

Her beast spoke up. *He won't be. Not if I have any say in it.*

No killing. You know that.

Her dragon sniffed. *I wouldn't waste the effort. Well, unless they hurt a child. Then I may have to teach them a lesson.*

The door at the other end of the room opened, and the rush of air brought forward a multitude of new scents.

One was a male scent she instantly recognized. Shane Farhall was here.

While he was intelligent enough not to speak, not disguising his smell meant Honoria could refine her plan for Shane specifically.

The soft footsteps of one person drew closer, until they had to be about halfway down the hall. Taking a deep breath, she rushed into Shane's line of sight and pretended to be nervous. "What are you doing here?"

Shane snarled, "What, is King hiding so that his bitch could protect him?"

Her dragon roared inside her head, but Honoria sent a quick warning to her beast to calm down before she replied in a deliberately wavering voice, "I can handle myself."

A cruel smirk curled the edges of Shane's mouth. The sight made her dragon want to cut off the male's cock, but thankfully her beast didn't try to wrestle control away from Honoria.

Shane stated, "Then let's see how far I can go without technically breaking any of the rules. It's about time you learned how females are too weak to lead, let alone be Protectors. There'll be none of that when I win this competition."

She swore she heard a growl behind her—although she didn't know if it was from Asher or Fraser—and decided to step forward, keeping Shane's focus on her for as long as possible. She still needed to find a way to let Asher know that Shane alone had come into the room. Only then could she make her dramatic move and have her partner help her.

For effect, she took a step back. "Where's your partner?"

"I don't need him to help me take you down, Wakeham. I'll do it myself. But before I do that, why don't you tell me where the Fraser bastard is? If you do, then I might go a little easier on you."

Wanting to prod him a little since Shane's temper always made him act more rash, she said, "Can't find him yourself,

I see. That's not what I'd call leader material."

Narrowing his eyes, Shane moved closer. "Says the female who spent too many years with that pansy clan in America. Dragons are stronger without the humans. I'll make sure the other leaders know that, in the end."

Her beast roared again, but Honoria was quick to answer Shane. She needed him a bit more unstable. "Once their fake hostage reports your actions, they won't pick you. Just because you win this round doesn't mean you win the whole thing."

"You say that, but if I mention how one of the other pairs ended up killing that Scottish arsehole and I found him that way, then no one will be the wiser."

At the intense hatred in Shane's eyes, Honoria drew in a breath. The dragonman wasn't sane, nor should he have made it this far. Even if the other leaders were merely trying to push all the participants with more competition, surely they would've read the signs and put more precautions into place to prevent extremes, such as murder, from happening.

Her dragon spoke up. *Take one more step back, and Asher will help. Let him know how far away Shane is, for reference.*

"Five feet is close enough, Shane. Stay back."

"Shut it, bitch. Tell me where the Scottish bastard is. The longer you take in answering me, the more pain you're going to feel."

For a split second, an actual thread of fear wormed its way into her heart. However, she wasn't going to tackle Shane alone. She knew that together, she and Asher would win.

They had to.

So instead of answering Shane, Honoria took yet another step back, signaling it was time for her partner to act.

And then all hell broke loose.

~~~

Only because Asher trusted Honoria did he fight his instinct to help her. Of course, when Fraser had growled at something Shane said, it'd nearly put their whole plan into jeopardy.

However, Honoria must've heard the growl, too, and adjusted her tactic. Even facing a dragonman who could probably kill her, she'd focused on letting Asher know Shane was alone before proceeding to poke his temper.

Even though she wasn't a warrior by training, Honoria knew how to keep herself together when push came to shove.

She'd make a fucking amazing leader.

His beast spoke up. *With us. Together, we work best.*

However, at that moment, Honoria finally reached the point in the room which signaled it was time for Asher to stop waiting and pounce. She ducked down as he sprang forward, and he roared as he tackled Shane to the ground.

As they rolled, pushed, and shoved, he didn't spare a thought as to if the others were doing their parts. He had faith in Honoria.

As Shane clawed his face, the feeling of talon against skin banished thoughts of his plan and instead reminded him of another time and place. One where he'd been strapped to a chair as two dragomen took turns carving a K into his chest before sealing the wound with hot metal.

However, instead of making him lose himself in the memory, this time it fueled his strength. Skyhunter deserved better than that. Shane would probably follow in Marcus King's footsteps, and fuck if he'd ever let that happen.

Shane Farhall would never be leader as long as he lived.

Never.
~~~

Wrestling the other male beneath him, Asher pressed his forearm against Shane's throat, pinning him in place. "I won't kill you, but are you ready to surrender?"

Shane gurgled his reply, "Never."

Talons dug into Asher's back, and he roared. However, he only increased the pressure against Shane's neck. Not to kill him, but hopefully to knock him out.

Digging his claws in deeper, Shane's face began to shift into his dragon one.

Fuck, maybe the male was insane. Asher threaded every bit of dominance he possessed into his voice as he said, "Stop it, Shane. You'll collapse the tunnel and kill us all."

The idiot continued shifting, wings starting to sprout from his back.

With a curse, Asher wrenched Shane's talons from his back, jumped away, and headed for the rear door. Honoria stood in the entrance, horror on her face as Shane continued shifting.

She moved aside and Asher dove into the next room. "Shut the door. Now."

Honoria and Fraser moved to do so, just locking it as a loud crash came from the other side. Asher waited to see if the door would hold against the sudden weight of earth from the cave-in. And while it creaked a few times, it didn't break or bust open.

He tried to sit up and cried out as intense, sharp pain exploded through his body. Without fighting for life or death, his body was telling him to take it easy.

Honoria appeared on one side and Fraser the other. Fraser spoke first. "Bloody hell, was he trying to kill you?"

Lowering her face closer to his, Honoria asked, "What are your injuries?"

The corner of his mouth ticked up. "Practical even now."

"Stop it, Ash. I can't help you if I don't know what's

wrong."

"He stabbed my back, but I don't know how badly." He turned, gritting his teeth against the pain, until he rested on his side. Even though his vision was beginning to swim, he added, "Sorry, Ria. I'm not going to be much help soon. But I know you can save us."

"Don't you even talk about leaving me. I'll poke your wounds if I have to."

"You won't..."

Unable to stay conscious any longer, the world turned black.

Tears threatened to fall, but Honoria managed to keep them back. Crying wouldn't help any of them.

Especially since the so-called emergency help button was useless so far underground—it relied on cell towers and she'd yet to see any kind of amplifier in the tunnels—which was something the coordinating team should've realized. Until they reached somewhere closer to the surface, they were truly on their own.

Trying not to panic at Asher falling unconscious, she ripped off his shirt and sucked in a breath. Shane had stabbed him several times, and it would be a miracle if he hadn't hit something vital.

Looking at Fraser, she threaded every bit of dominance into her voice she could muster. "What are the back-up protocols for this place?"

The defiance from earlier was gone as Fraser replied without missing a beat. "Assuming the Protectors watching the place have been compromised, then the other only fallback is a secret tunnel, the entrance to which is in the next room. It should lead to a room full of emergency support staff."

"Then fetch them."

Fraser didn't move. "Not until we move him into the next room, just in case the weight of the dirt breaks the door. Whoever that dragonman was, he was bloody insane."

Not wanting to think about the dragonman who might've mortally wounded Asher, she motioned toward her partner's upper half. "You carry the front and I'll take the legs."

Somehow they managed to get Asher into the next room. While there wasn't a bed, there was a table and they gently laid Asher on his stomach.

The second he was settled, she forced herself to look away from Asher's injuries and she pierced Fraser with an urgent look. "Where's this door?"

The Scot went to the side and tapped around a certain area on the wall until a panel clicked. He slid it open and cursed. "There should be someone on the other side of this door. This doesn't look good, lass."

A loud creak emanated from the next room. Not good. It could burst at any moment. "Do you have any medical experience?"

"Afraid not. I'm an architect by trade."

"Damn." She glanced at Asher's pale face. "Let's try to clean him up and wrap a tight bandage around his torso, to help keep it from bleeding even more."

Fraser motioned toward a derelict metal cabinet in one corner. "There are a few things in here." He went to the cabinet and opened the drawer. "A small first-aid kit, some water, and some high-energy snacks."

"Bring the kit and water. Hell, bring the snacks too. I don't think Ash is waking up anytime soon, but in case he does, he'll need the calories to heal faster."

Dragon-shifters healed quickly, but they didn't possess magic, nor were they miracle workers. Asher could still die.

Her beast spoke up. *He's too stubborn to die. Especially since the sex score is still in our favor. He'll wake up to make a comeback, I'm sure.*

Grateful for her dragon's attempt to lighten the mood a little, Honoria banished her fears and went to work cleaning Asher's injuries as best she could.

Once done, she went over to the open door between the room next to the cave-in and their location, closed it and locked it. "At least that should be another barrier to hopefully protect us." Turning to Fraser, she added, "Now, we need to find help. How long is that tunnel? And what's on the other side?"

"It's quite long, I'm afraid. And if that crazy bastard didn't harm the others down here, then protocols say they should be in one of the three meeting rooms dotted along the length of the tunnel."

Honoria nodded. "We need to go and hopefully find them."

Her glance drifted to Asher's still form. It would be better if she and Fraser went looking for the others together, but that meant leaving him behind.

And Honoria didn't want to do it. He could die, and he didn't deserve to die alone.

Her beast spoke up. *Stop with the dying nonsense. He's strong. After surviving five years as a prisoner, he's not going to give up now.*

Just because you say it doesn't make it so.

We have to believe. Otherwise, if we split up from the Scottish dragonman and he runs into Shane's partner, who knows what will happen to the male. And if he doesn't reach the meeting rooms, then it'd spell all of our doom.

Her dragon was correct.

Leaning down to Asher's ear, she said, "I won't be gone long, I promise. And you'd better be fine when I get back. I have a thing or two to say to you." Her voice softened. "One of them is thank you, by the way."

Kissing his forehead gave her the courage to stand and look at Fraser. She ordered, "Lead the way and let's find help."

Twenty minutes later, Honoria clenched her fingers as they exited the second meeting room. They hadn't found another soul yet, and each minute that ticked by was another that could take Asher's life.

However, she knew yelling at Fraser wouldn't accomplish anything, so they quickly kept moving along the tunnel, keeping all of their senses on alert for the slightest change.

Her beast spoke up. *Can't we use the emergency button yet to call for help?*

I think we're still too far underground, and I haven't seen anything to boost or transmit the signal, not even in the meeting rooms. I didn't even see a blasted telephone in one of the rooms.

If we get close enough to use the button or make a call, will you do it?

Yes. The leadership isn't worth Asher's life.

Her beast hummed. *I agree. Maybe once he's healed and healthy again, you'll consider taking him as our mate.*

She liked how her beast didn't say *if* Asher pulled through. While it was always a possibility he wouldn't, she believed positive thoughts helped in some way.

A tapping suddenly echoed through the tunnel. She and Fraser both stilled. There was a pattern to the sound, but even with the little Morse code she'd learned as a child, she recognized it as something different.

Fraser stood a little taller and flashed a grin. "That's Gregor. Come on."

She kept up with Fraser's pace. "Who?"

"Dr. Gregor Innes. He was Lochguard's head doctor until he mated a female dragon-shifter on Stonefire. But that code is something Clan Lochguard developed for emergencies. It's brilliant because it's nonsense to anyone else, but it spells out words to me."

"Tell me it's good news."

He nodded. "It's basically a call out for any Lochguard participants to go to the third meeting room, the one we haven't seen yet. We should find at least one doctor there."

A small sliver of hope filled her heart. "We need to hurry then, so Dr. Innes can help Asher. And while I'm not grateful, what about the others not from Scotland? Will they just be left to fend on their own?"

Honoria was thinking of the teenage girl who had tested her earlier. Her accent had marked her as Welsh.

Fraser started to run. She kept pace as he answered, "Of course not, that's ridiculous. Each clan in the UK has their own code. Well, it seems except for Skyhunter. I'm sure everyone takes a turn from the respective clans, letting people know where to go."

"Having a universal one would be easier."

"Aye, maybe now. But keep in mind, we all were enemies not that long ago."

She didn't think Fraser was intentionally taking a stab at Skyhunter, but it still stung.

Her dragon spoke up. *But no longer. The others will come along soon enough.*

I wish I could say yes, but given the chaos of this test, the DDA could still decide Skyhunter isn't stable enough and disband us.

Then we'll fight it. Skyhunter is worth saving. It's home again.

Fraser rounded a corner and then skidded to a halt in front of a large metal door with signs of rust. He tapped out something on the door, someone tapped back, and he did it again, too. While the exchange couldn't have taken more than thirty seconds, each tap made Honoria more impatient. Asher could be dying, and the doctor who could help him was busy doing some complicated code.

Honoria's temper didn't flare often, but it threatened to do so.

However, the door finally opened to reveal a tall man about forty, with blond hair. He spoke with a Scottish accent, "Fraser." He looked over. "And Honoria. I'm Dr. Innes. Where's your partner?"

She didn't waste a second. "Asher was injured and fell unconscious. Please, you need to come back with us and help him. He might be dying."

A younger female with short, dark hair stepped next to Dr. Innes. She spoke with a Northern English accent. "No one is going without me. I'm Brenna. We can do longer introductions later, but I'm a Protector."

Her dragon perked up at that. *A female Protector. They do exist.*

Of course they do. Hush.

"Fine, the whole bloody room can come, if that's what it takes." She threaded dominance into her voice. "But let's go. Now. I won't have Asher die because a few people decided that chitchat was more important."

Brenna smiled and moved into the tunnel, in front of them all. "I like you already. Come on, I know where all the rooms are along this tunnel and will make sure it's still safe."

Honoria started running, hoping the doctor would keep up. She couldn't help but spit out to Brenna, "Why are you all bloody hiding in that room? Surely you know part of the tunnel collapsed and we needed your help."

Brenna didn't miss a beat. "The cameras were disabled and we had to manually go through the rooms. Most of the Protectors are busy keeping one of the rule-breaking males under their watch. I couldn't leave the others unless there was a known emergency. We didn't think so many Protectors were necessary."

"I think there were a lot of screw-ups regarding this whole thing." She told Brenna about Shane, the fight, and shifting inside the tunnel before asking, "Who thought using abandoned tunnels would be a good idea?"

Brenna shook her head. "There was no way to know some stupid bloody dragonman would be idiotic enough to shift inside a tunnel. If someone made it this far in the trials and was that insane, then that's on the others testing you lot."

"But aren't you from Stonefire, too?"

"Sort of. I belong to Stonefire, but my mate is the brother of Clan Glenlough's leader. I sometimes work for both of them, depending on need."

Glenlough was the clan in Ireland run by the female dragon-shifter, Teagan O'Shea.

Brenna continued before Honoria could say anything. "Technically, clans from the Republic of Ireland weren't allowed to help with all this. However, I'm originally from Stonefire, so it was a way in for my sister-in-law, too. Teagan, Bram, and Finn all want to strengthen bonds between the dragon clans in the future, and who ends up leading Skyhunter is vital to all of that. So, that's why I'm here."

She sensed there was more of a story behind her explanation, but they finally reached back to where Honoria and Fraser had started their search, and she pushed aside her curiosity. Honoria moved in front of Brenna. "Let me check first. If Asher is awake and sees an unfamiliar face, he may attack you."

Brenna studied her a second before nodding. "Okay. But I'll be right behind you."

The doctor finally caught up to them, but Honoria felt around the wall until she found the latch for the secret door. She slowly opened it until she could see into the room. Asher sat up on the table, his head barely off his chest.

He was alive.

"Asher!" She pushed the door open and ran to his side. His eyes found hers and the pain she saw there twisted her heart. "Ssh, I have a doctor. He'll be able to help you."

Dr. Innes moved next to her and started checking Asher's wounds. Honoria took a step back, but Asher reached out a hand and grabbed hers. His voice was low as he said, "Don't leave me, Ria."

"Never, Asher. I'll never leave you."

And while some may think it was just the intensity of the situation making her say anything, Honoria meant it. They may be older and different people, but she loved him as much—if not more—than when she'd been a teenager.

The only question was whether they would still have a chance at ruling together, or if Asher's injuries crippled him and he would no longer be considered.

Her beast growled. *Don't think like that. The doctor is here. We did all the coordinators asked, and more. The other dragon leaders at least should realize that.*

Honoria still had her doubts, but she managed to hide it from her dragon. Instead, she kept Asher's hand in hers the whole time the doctor helped him, letting Asher know how much she cared for him with her eyes.

What she wouldn't give for some time alone with her dragonman. However, she had a feeling that would be a long time coming.

Chapter Ten

It was days before Asher was both awake and alone with Honoria. The bloody Scottish doctor kept running tests, barring visitors most of the time, and had even kept Asher unconscious for an entire day so his body could heal faster.

And what snippets he had seen of Honoria had always been in the company of others. Which meant he still hadn't had the chance to haul her close—pain be damned—and kiss her like there was no tomorrow.

Except they'd agreed to no public displays of affection and he wouldn't break his word. However, if he could get a bloody minute alone with her, maybe he could renegotiate. That would satisfy his randy beast, always banging out about their female.

Not that he didn't want Honoria, too. But his human side understood Skyhunter's dire straits. For all he knew, there may not be a Skyhunter to live on in the near future. And he wanted one, even if he didn't end up leading it. More than anything, he wanted to settle down with Honoria and make a fresh start.

Asher must've not kept that thought private, and his dragon grunted. *She should be ours. I don't understand why you keep coming up with ways to delay it. Even if we can't claim her with our cock, we could do it with kissing or words.*

He could toe the line and say it was more important to talk with the other clan leaders and the DDA. They still hadn't found out what would happen to Skyhunter since no one had bothered to let him or anyone else know yet.

However, he burned to talk with his female.

Yes, his. After lying there, barely remaining conscious as Honoria talked with him back in the tunnel, he'd admitted to himself how he loved her again, far more than when he'd been a teenager. And as his vision had swum and faded to black, his last thought had been that he'd never be able to tell her the truth.

He replied, *I do want to claim her, but there's a time and place, dragon. We're not about to die. We have time.*

His dragon grunted. *I don't understand your human way of thinking. Regardless, she should be here by now. If Ria doesn't come soon, we won't get any time alone with her. Again.*

Her text saying she would be here only came a few minutes ago.

The door opened, silencing both man and beast.

Honoria had her hair pulled up, showing off her graceful neck and a jaw Asher wanted to nibble. The tight top highlighted her curves, as did the jeans slung low on her hips.

What he wouldn't give to get her out of those clothes.

She smiled at him and walked up to his bed. "You're awake and not scowling. That's a good start."

His dragon snorted. *If she looked down, she'd see why we aren't scowling.*

Shut it, dragon.

As his beast cackled, he focused on his female. He took her hand and kissed the back of it, barely noticing the slight twinges in his back as he did so. Her soft, warm skin under his lips only made his cock harder.

It seemed certain parts of him were in perfect working order.

He finally replied, "Excuse me for my earlier scowling. I only, you know, received over a dozen stab wounds. Ones that are still healing, by the way."

She raised a golden eyebrow. "I showered plenty of sympathy on you the first few days. But you're healing well, so stop milking it for everything it's worth."

The corner of his mouth ticked up. "There are so many things I love about you, Ria."

While the comment was casual, Asher realized he wanted to say more than he loved aspects of Ria. No, he loved the female in front of him. For her courage, strength, humor, and so much more.

His beast hummed. *Then tell her.*

Given his recent ordeal, as well as his five-year prison stint, Asher tried to seize the moments he could. He, more than most anyone, knew tomorrow wasn't guaranteed.

And yet, as Honoria stood next to his bed and stared into his eyes, the chance ripe for the plucking, his tongue lay heavy in his mouth.

His dragon sniffed. *Why? She could be ours. Just tell her. I'm sure she feels the same way.*

Honoria's voice prevented his reply. "So what does Mr. Dragon have to say?"

His beast growled. *Tell her.*

Asher grunted. "Just being bossy, as usual."

Honoria grinned, and her beauty made his heart skip a beat. He wanted her. Not just for sex—which he couldn't wait to be healed for again, for sure—but also as his mate. Everything was better, easier, brighter when she was near.

She replied, "You may not like it, but I find it amusing.

Big, bad Asher who managed to survive multiple stab wounds and somehow not have anything vital damaged most certainly needs some humility. Otherwise, you might think you're invincible."

He raised an eyebrow, one of the few parts of his body that didn't hurt to move. "I'm not fifteen and out to prove I'm a grown male. I'm well aware I'm not invincible." He took her hand and squeezed. "But let's not joke around right now. Someone could walk through that door at any time and there are things we should talk about."

She searched his eyes. "What do you want to tell me, Ash?"

His heart beat faster. This was it. He needed to tell Honoria he wanted her as his mate. And even if it was too soon for her, then maybe they could at least try living together so he could convince her how right it was.

Just as he opened his mouth to take the plunge, the Scottish dragonman Dr. Innes waltzed into the room, followed by the Stonefire and Lochguard leaders.

Asher's life seemed cursed with bad timing.

However, the gaggle of males started talking before he could get in a word edgewise.

Honoria's time alone with Asher had lasted no more than a few minutes, her not even being able to kiss him once, before someone else barged in.

Someone always seemed to be barging in.

If she were actually clan leader, then she wouldn't mind as much. At least in that case there would be a reason and purpose behind all the interruptions.

But she swore people kept popping their heads in to ensure they were both still there and alive. While she hadn't heard anything about dangers to them or others inside the clan, maybe some kind of threat had come from Shane Farhall's partner. The male was currently detained and in the hands of the Protectors.

Her beast spoke up. *I hope he finally told everyone the extent of his and Shane's betrayal.*

I wish I knew. Being kept in the dark is crap. Even if we aren't allowed to become the leaders, I just want to know what the hell is going on.

Her beast sniffed. *They still don't trust us.*

Maybe. But if you were the DDA or the other dragon leaders, could you blame them?

Before her dragon could reply, Dr. Innes grunted and his voice filled the room. "I think it's still too early for Asher to deal with visitors such as you two."

Finn's brow rose as if offended. "Och, come on, Innes. I'm the most charming male you know."

Bram sighed. "No, we're not getting into this again." He moved his gaze to the doctor. "It'll be short and to the point. Besides, the monitors will let you know if his health is in any danger."

The doctor grunted again, a bit louder this time. "Fine. But if you worsen his condition in any way, then I'll pull my rank as doctor and order you out until I say otherwise."

While it was true doctors were one of the few members of a dragon clan who could order the clan leader about, Honoria never remembered anyone telling Marcus King what to do. It was fascinating to watch.

Her dragon chimed in, *I'm sure once we have a new head doctor here, they can be coaxed to do the same.*

Even if they weren't the leaders was left unsaid.

With one last glare at Bram and Finn, Dr. Innes exited the room.

Asher jumped in before anyone else could. "Let's not repeat the last time we met and have you two joke around and take your time getting to the point. Just tell us what you need to say."

The corner of Bram's mouth ticked up. "No sugarcoating, I see. That's good because what I have to say isn't easy."

Honoria's stomach twisted in knots. She had no idea if Bram would tell them that Skyhunter was to be disbanded; or maybe he'd inform them of how they hadn't won the right to lead; or possibly something much worse than she could even imagine. Regardless, none of the options were good.

But at least she might finally be able to hear Skyhunter's fate.

Bram continued, "Your clan is on rocky ground, much like before. That idiot Farhall killed himself and injured a few of our people with his shifting inside a tunnel." He shook his head. "Who shifts in a fucking tunnel?"

Honoria pointed out, "You put us there, so remember that."

"Aye, we did," Bram stated.

Finn jumped in. "Keeping the crazy arsehole in the running was a mistake, just like I said. Maybe next time you'll stand with me, Bram, instead of siding with the other leaders and even the DDA."

Bram put up a hand. "You can argue with me about that later. I don't want to linger or risk Innes's wrath." He focused back on Honoria and Asher. "Even though the DDA originally wanted to disband Skyhunter as a result of the chaotic, dangerous outcome of the trials, we convinced them to give Skyhunter one last chance." He pointed to each of them. "You two, in fact, are getting that chance. It'll be your job to clean things up and start showing progress with the clan. If you can't meet set deadlines or goals, then the DDA will rethink the disbandment decision, and no amount of talking from me or my colleagues will change their minds."

Honoria's dragon stood tall inside her mind. *I knew we could do it.*

Ignoring her beast, she shared a glance with Asher. Even though there was a crapton of stuff to do, she couldn't help but smile. "We did it."

However, if she was hoping for a smile, it didn't come. Asher's brows came together. "When does this start?"

"Now," Bram answered. "Innes won't like it, but already your clan members are talking about what happened with Farhall. Leave them leaderless for even a week to let you heal, and I guarantee people will be stirring panic and maybe even fleeing in droves. Not that I don't like having more people in my clan, but I'd rather have an ally down here, in the south. Because if not, the dragon hunters will pounce on the opening and grow like weeds in the southern counties. And that's not something I want to deal with."

A million thoughts raced through Honoria's head, but she forced herself to nod and reply, "Then we'll deal with it." She looked back at Asher. "When will you be strong enough to address the clan jointly?"

"This evening."

It was on the tip of her tongue to say no bloody way, but rationally, she knew Asher was nearly healed. He might have some physical therapy in his near future, but he could walk a few paces and stand for ten minutes.

Not that she was going to like watching her male suffer at all.

Her dragon spoke up. *He's suffered worse. He's strong and will do what's needed.*

Asher spoke up again. "Now if you two could set up everything with the Protectors to have a clan meeting tonight, we could do with some time alone."

Finn winked. "Aye, I suspect you do."

Not wanting her cheeks to burn in front of the Scottish leader, she merely nodded her parting. Once the pair was gone, she turned to Asher. "We did it. The truth's still setting in, but we did it."

He patted the bed, and she sat next to him. Taking her hand, he kissed the back of it. "Yes, we did. And while I'm prepared to spend almost every waking hour getting Skyhunter back on track, right now I need to kiss you, Ria. Come here."

Since moving his torso could still be painful and trigger a spasm in his back, Honoria leaned over until her lips were a hairbreadth from his. Staring into his eyes, the heat and triumph there making her skin burn in a good way, it hit her. Asher would be her partner to lead the clan, but she wanted more than that.

Honoria wanted him as her best friend, her lover, her partner in all things.

The urge to let him know bubbled up inside her. Her beast hummed. *Tell him. Now. While we have the chance. He is ours, and he should know it.*

Before she could stop herself, she murmured, "I love you, Asher King."

With a growl, Asher closed the distance and kissed her.

~~~

Asher wished he was whole and hearty for many reasons. The clan—correction, his and Honoria's clan—needed a lot of work and care before they could rein it in and make it thrive again. Not to mention they would need to start forming temporary alliances with various leaders as soon as possible, no matter how annoying they may be.
~~~

However, right after Honoria said she loved him, Asher wanted to be healthy so he could claim his female and tell her he felt the same way.

He wanted her, needed her, was starting to have trouble imagining a future without her.

Since he couldn't claim her yet without possibly making his injuries worse, Asher risked the slight twinges to close the distance between their lips and kiss her.

She opened immediately, and he took his time stroking, tasting, and exploring her mouth. Each lick sent heat rushing through his body, straight to his cock.

His dragon hummed. *She could ride us. That wouldn't hurt us or worsen our condition.*

We can't. Not until the clan is settled.

Yes, we can. Later. Everyone needs a break sometimes.

Wanting to treasure his female as much as possible, Asher ignored his dragon and pulled Honoria closer. Even though it'd been less than a week since he'd had her naked in his arms, it seemed like years.

Fuck, he wanted her more than anything. Maybe even the leadership.

But as her fingers brushed the K-shaped scar on his chest, memories of everything that had happened under his uncle's reign came rushing back.

The pain, the manipulation, the fear. Families being torn apart, lives taken for petty reasons, and so much more.

He couldn't let that happen ever again.

As he pulled back, Honoria searched his gaze. "What's wrong?"

"I want you to know that I love you, Ria. And I wish I could claim you right here and now, forgetting the outside world, and creating our own bubble of happiness. But we can't. The scar on my chest is a reminder of what happened, and I never want that to repeat. Ever. So forgive me, love. I need to not kiss and cherish you for a bit, until we get things a little more settled."

Honoria smiled, the sight warming his heart. "That was a rather long-winded way to tell me you love me."

He frowned. "That's what you got from that? Did you miss the part when I said I'll probably have to neglect and ignore you for a while, until things are more under control and we're not teetering on the precipice of disbandment?"

She stroked the hair at his forehead, the warmth of her fingers soothing away his negative emotions. "We knew what we were getting into. And I agree, the clan will have to come first for a bit." She leaned down until her hot breath tickled his ear. "But we have to take care of ourselves, too, Ash. Tell me again how you love me."

His voice was husky to his own ears as he said, "I love you, Honoria Wakeham. Far more than any teenage boy ever could have. And as soon as I can, I'll prove it to you every way I know how."

Her smile widened. "That's all that matters, and I can wait for as long as needed." She kissed him slowly, and he let her take control for a few seconds. Pulling back, she added, "And maybe it's good we can't go at it full force for a bit. I'm not sure I can hold my dragon back, and the last thing we need is for you to be injured again."

He snorted. "Broken by dragon lust probably wouldn't go over well with the doctor."

"Probably not." She kissed him again. "But just know that I'm thinking of every way I can take you as soon as we have time and you're healthy. Some of my dragon's ideas may even make your beast blush."

His dragon huffed. *She can't scare me. Now I have to think of dirtier things to do to her.*

He laughed. "Great, now there's a competition between our beasts for who can be the dirtiest. We may not get much of a say in the matter until they settle it."

"Hmm, we'll see about that. However, my dragon knows how I'll be the first to claim the man I love, not her."

Hear that, dragon? I'm going to do the same.

His beast grunted. *We'll see about that.*

Dr. Innes burst into the room. The bloody male kept doing that, to the point Asher wondered if he had cameras in the room, alerting him to when a patient may be tempted to do something they shouldn't.

Honoria never moved from her position next to him, though. And the act made him love her even more.

As he rubbed circles on Honoria's back—fuck the no display of public affection just then—she spoke up. "Yes, doctor? We haven't broken any of your rules, and Asher is fine, so I'm not sure why you're here."

Dr. Innes rolled his eyes. "Aye, you'll fit right in as leader. I think it's a bloody requirement for them to be stubborn and test my patience."

Asher cleared his throat. "What do you need, Dr. Innes?"

The other male answered, "The other two leaders mentioned how you'll be needing out of this room today. So I'm here to do a final check and give you stern instructions about your recovery, which I'm sure you won't follow."

Since Asher had lost too much time in prison as it was, he didn't beat around the bush if he could help it. "I'm not stupid, but I'll push boundaries. Tell me what I absolutely can't do without risking a relapse, or worse, permanent damage."

The other male didn't miss a beat. "No flying, end of story. I'm not sure how the damage to your back will affect your wings in dragon form. The first time you shift, I want to be there."

After so many years of not being able to fly, the thought of being earthbound again for an unknown amount of time didn't sit well with him. "I won't, but when can I try?"

Dr. Innes glanced between the pair. "We'll see, aye? I suspect you'll be busy with clan matters for a wee while anyway. All I ask is that you keep an open line of communication with me. If I call or text, you answer. You don't do that—barring some clan emergency—then I will station a Protector with you at all times to act as my liaison. And they won't be from this clan, either, so they'll listen to my authority over yours."

Honoria jumped in and asked, "You're a tough one, aren't you?"

The doctor raised his blond brows. "When you deal with clan leaders, you have to be."

Even though he may not want to follow Dr. Innes's orders to the letter, he admired the male for his dedication. At that thought, he had an idea. "What would you say to helping us pick a head doctor for Skyhunter?"

Gregor blinked. "Oh, aye? Are you sure about that? I already get the sense the people here don't like outsiders."

Honoria chimed in, "No, I think it's a brilliant idea. Ash and I will make the final decision, but we need to appoint someone who's dedicated and will risk ordering us about, like you've been doing, when needed."

Dr. Innes bobbed his head. "I'm interested, but can I bring my mate into this to help me? She's probably had more interaction with the other English dragon-shifter doctors than I have. And I think, for the time being, your clan will trust an English dragon-shifter over ones from other parts of the UK."

Dr. Innes's mate was also a doctor. Not just any doctor, but Stonefire's head doctor. She was back on Stonefire, unable to travel because of her pregnancy.

He and Honoria nodded at one another before Asher replied, "Your mate is well-known even down here. If she helps, it'll be an even better choice, I'm sure."

The corner of Dr. Innes's mouth ticked up. "Don't tell her that, aye? Otherwise, I'll never hear the end of it."

After finishing his final check and giving a few more orders—Ash was to limit any intense physical activity for a few more days—the Scottish doctor left.

Meeting Honoria's gaze, he asked, "So, are you ready to get to work?"

She kissed him and answered, "More than anything. Our first meeting tonight will be extremely important. So we're going to have to stop kissing and touching to focus on it. Not that I want to, of course, but if we don't nail this and start stirring confidence or earning trust, our leadership may be doomed before it even begins."

He agreed. And while Asher did his best to work on the speech and coordinate how they'd run the meeting, he did steal a few kisses here and there. After all, distractions helped to reboot the brain at times.

And he couldn't wait until he could do more than distract his dragonwoman. Asher looked forward to when he could steal her away and become her whole world for a few hours.

Chapter Eleven

Before the clan-wide meeting in the great hall on Skyhunter, Honoria and Asher had met with the Protectors first. Since Asher had remained on Skyhunter and knew who had been loyal to the clan and who had chosen to side with Marcus King, Honoria had deferred to him selecting the head Protector, Robin Driscoll.

Asher and Robin had been imprisoned together, and more importantly, had both survived mostly intact. Even if Robin and Honoria had never interacted much as youths, his trust in Asher was absolute. Meaning, if Asher trusted her at his side, Robin would, too. And between Robin and Asher's support of her, others had warmed to the quasi-outsider being anointed their leader by the DDA's mandate.

Robin was now at the back of the great hall, waiting for their signal. Honoria and Asher's first joint meeting was going to be flashy for a reason—to show they would be doing things in the open, allowing others to disagree with them without fear of punishment.

Well, as long as their disagreements didn't cause harm. The clan may already know about them being the new leaders, but it would be the first time Honoria and Asher met them all as such. She didn't think violence would erupt, and she hoped their plans for the evening would help prevent or discourage it.

Her dragon paced inside Honoria's mind. *What's with all the dramatics? Dragons like honesty. That should be enough.*

But the human halves want a leader who is more than your average person, hence adding a little dramatic flair.

If you say so.

Asher touched her arm and she glanced over. He murmured, "Ready?"

"Are you?"

He smiled. "Probably a bit less so since all I think about is wanting out of this blasted brace around my waist."

"Don't even think about taking it off. The muscles in your back aren't at full strength. Wearing the brace means you can stand longer than without it. And even if we don't plan on this meeting taking hours, it might go long, and I hardly think a clan leader lying prostrate on the floor will instill confidence."

"I wouldn't be on the bloody floor. We're fancy here on Skyhunter and have chairs now."

She narrowed her eyes. But before she could make a retort, Asher lowered his voice even further, to the point only she could hear it. "However, I'll keep it on. That way when the brace does come off, I can lay back, take it easy, and let you and your dragon take charge."

Her beast growled. *I'll take him up on his offer. So hurry and conduct this meeting as fast as you can so I can ride him hard.*

Hush. This can't be rushed.

But I want him.

You just want to beat his dragon.

No. Both human and dragon halves belong to us. I want to claim Asher and make it official.

Since her dragon would keep trying to make her case, Honoria focused back on Asher. She shrugged. "So you must mean I can tuck you in, say goodnight, walk away, and have you follow my orders, then yes, we can do that."

"Cheeky female."

She winked. "Always."

Asher chuckled, and the sound made her insides flip. He would never be the same male from over a decade ago, and she accepted it. But it was nice to hear him laugh again. She'd just have to try and make him do it more often.

Her beast huffed. *That is another human thing. Fuck him often, and he'll be happy.*

Honoria choked back a laugh and just in time as the clock outside the great hall chimed the hour. A few beats later, the main doors to the hall opened.

Taking a deep breath, Honoria stood tall and watched as the members of her clan filed in.

Yes, her clan. Well, hers and Asher's. Still, her heart skipped a beat at that thought. Skyhunter was indeed home again, and now it was up to her and Asher to make sure it survived.

Asher lightly touched her arm for support. They had both decided to keep their public displays of affection to when they were alone for the time being. Well, unless they trusted the people they were with not to use it against them. Otherwise, if they were open about their nonworking relationship with everyone, many of the clan members might start doubting Skyhunter's future, especially if their relationship fell to pieces.

Her dragon growled. *It won't.*

I don't think so either. But remember, these people have had a rough time of it. And that's an understatement, to say the least.

Falling silent, her beast curled up at the back of her mind, the usual pose that meant she'd keep quiet and let Honoria settle the human things she didn't always understand.

Roughly three hundred sets of eyes ranging from tiny babies to grizzled, gray-haired great-grandparents stared at her and Asher. While only clan members were allowed on the hall floor, the other dragon-shifter leaders, as well as the DDA personnel, were watching from a secret room on the second floor, overlooking the space.

In other words, Asher and Honoria needed to impress everyone who mattered from the get-go.

Her and Asher had gone back and forth about who should speak first, weighing the pros and cons from every angle. In the end, they'd decided she should open the meeting.

Honoria stepped forward, watching everyone's face closely as she did so. Her speaking before Asher might stir the pot, but it was something they needed to do. If the people before her couldn't accept a female being in charge, then they'd have to be addressed as quickly as possible.

Raising a hand for silence, it fell quiet almost instantly. Given the meetings she remembered as a child, which had always taken several minutes to get into order, the action spoke volumes about how important this moment in time really was.

Honoria carefully projected her voice, to ensure everyone heard what she had to say. "Thank you for coming on such short notice. I'm sure everyone has a lot of questions, or even maybe a few doubts, but Asher and I wanted to welcome everyone to Skyhunter 2.0. While some changes will be rolled out slowly, others will be happening as soon as possible. The goal is to make the clan more than a place to live. We want to make it home again, a place where a person wants to be rather than one where someone remains simply because they have nowhere else to go."

Asher jumped in before anyone from the crowd could ask a question. "Which brings us straight to the first point. Unlike the previous regime, no one is going to force you to remain here. If you wish to leave the clan permanently, you can." He waved toward the door. "In fact, if you aren't even going to give us a chance, then feel free to leave now. The DDA will even help you relocate to somewhere else. We'll give you sixty seconds to exit and leave us, starting now."

He signaled to Robin, who opened both of the giant doors to the hall. Murmurs went up in the crowd, but Honoria merely stood and waited. Some would be against a female being in charge, even if only partially, and this was the best way to get rid of them now.

A few of the older dragon-shifters shuffled out, as did one young couple she didn't recognize.

At the end of sixty seconds, Robin blared a horn and the doors closed again, thanks to the Protectors outside.

It was Honoria's turn again. "Right, with that out of the way, let's get down to answering the questions on everyone's mind. Yes, there are two of us. And yes, others will be acting as liaisons for various things to help us keep the clan running smoothly. However, your opinions are welcome and will be heard. We can't guarantee anything—after all, if someone suggests painting all the homes bright pink, I can't imagine Asher would agree to it—but we'll be fair."

Smiles broke on some of the faces, and it boosted Honoria's confidence. Her first attempt at proving she and Asher were different than the previous leader had worked.

Her dragon rolled her eyes but remained quiet. Any distraction, no matter how much she loved her beast, would be bad form at the moment.

Asher's voice filled the hall. "Some of you may be hesitant about my surname being King." He paused to tug off his shirt. Given how much Asher hated showing the scar on his pec, it proved to Honoria he'd do anything for the clan. Asher continued, "I'm sure everyone's seen the K on my chest. I was imprisoned and tortured for speaking out against Marcus's policies. For five long years, I endured it all to prove how much I disapproved of him, never caving. Not even when this brand was seared into my chest did I agree with his ruthless ways. If this scar on my chest isn't enough proof to show how different I am, then I hope you will at least give me a chance. I don't need absolute loyalty as the former leader did, but if anyone does something to threaten Skyhunter's survival, then we'll deal with it promptly."

He paused to survey the room slowly. Honoria didn't flinch at Asher's stern looks, but a few of the people in the audience did a double-take. No doubt, they were contrasting Asher now to the carefree teenager he'd once been.

Not that it was a bad change. Honoria rather liked his serious side at times.

Only once he'd scanned the entire room did he continue. "Also, Skyhunter won't be isolated from the other clans in the UK any longer. Working together is important, especially as dragon-shifters have enemies across the entire UK. While we're a tough bunch of dragons, a full-out assault from either the dragon hunters or Dragon Knights could bring us to our knees without allies."

There were a few murmurs, but Honoria couldn't tell if they were good or bad ones.

Together, they would need to find some community liaisons to help gauge the clan's moods. She added it to her ever-growing list of things to do.

Asher stared until the noise died down. "And lastly, we'll never be allowed to participate in the sacrifice program, either, to help rebuild our population until the Department of Dragon Affairs is convinced we're a safe, stable group of dragons. Which means *all* of our goals should be the same—to make Skyhunter the best dragon clan in the UK. Given our competition, it won't be easy, but I think we can do it."

Honoria had expected a few claps, but cheers rose up from the crowd. Looking from nods, to smiles, to even a few skeptical gazes, Honoria let out a breath. They were far from perfect, and there was still a long way to go before Skyhunter reached its potential, but the reaction was a good start. Because from a few seeds of hope, maybe trust and prosperity would bloom.

Her dragon grunted, wanting to comment. But she kept her promise to stay silent.

After a minute, Honoria raised her hand and the noise died down again. "We'll move into the leader's cottage by tomorrow and will open our doors as soon as possible to hear grievances or concerns. But there is one more thing we want to do right away, and that's get to know the other clans in the UK. Lochguard and Stonefire have offered to throw us a celebration banquet and dance next week, and we've accepted. It will allow you to mingle with some of the other clans, maybe meet someone with similar interests, or even someone with knowledge you can use for your own efforts here. But we can talk of business and what needs to be done soon enough. For a few days, settle down, take a deep breath, and start planning your future. Because if Asher and I have our way, it'll be a bright one."

People clapped, although not quite as enthusiastically as earlier. No doubt, they were nervous about meeting dragon-shifters from other parts of the UK. After all, Marcus King had spent almost two decades demonizing them every chance he had.

Her dragon raised her head. *But we can fix it.*

Asher dismissed the crowd, assuring them they would take questions as soon as possible. Robin and his Protectors efficiently escorted everyone out of the hall.

Once it was just them and Robin, Honoria leaned over and kissed Asher. "You did brilliantly."

"So did you."

"And fewer people chose to leave the clan than I had guessed. Although, I don't think it's a bad thing."

Bram's voice echoed in the hall, letting them know the others had come down from the second floor. "Aye, it went well. But the true test will be the celebration next week. Speaking of which, Finn and I are going to return home until then. I suspect it'll be easier to get things going without us breathing down your necks."

Finn snorted. "That's a nice cover story. I know you just want to go home to your mate."

Bram frowned. "Of course I do. But there's a rational reason, too."

Honoria jumped in before Finn could reply. "The reasons don't matter. I think it'll be easier to get a feel for the clan if you two aren't here." She sought out the DDA female's gaze. "And while I know you don't take orders from us, you leaving would also be a big help."

The human didn't hesitate to bob her head. "I agree. And the fact you didn't order me to leave already raises my opinion of you slightly." The human's face turned serious. "However, I want to impart how delicate Skyhunter's status is with the DDA. I know there will be small rumbles, but if it becomes out of control, we may have no choice but to break up the clan and seize the lands."

Honoria's dragon growled, but she replied to the human before her dragon started ranting. "We understand. I only hope you'll give us a fair chance."

The human nodded. "I will. Now, I should probably head off and start making my report—the trials themselves have created a mountain of paperwork. However, don't hesitate to reach out to me. I know some DDA employees see dragon-shifters as a liability, but I think they can be allies. Maybe one day, we can work closely together."

Asher grunted at her side, but Honoria smiled widely. "We'd like that."

The human made her goodbyes, leaving them alone with Finn, Bram, and Robin. Finn spoke first. "We'll be going in just a second. But I'll impart one piece of wisdom before I go. I, too, had to deal with a difficult transition when I took over Lochguard. However, with hard work and love for your people, it does get easier. Well, most of the time. I'm sure you remember my cousin Fraser, aye? Family doesn't always follow orders like they should."

At the mention of family, Honoria's longing for her absent cousins surged forth. Maybe if she tried hard enough, she could get them to come to the celebration next week.

Bram slapped Finn on the shoulder. "You can offer more advice next week. Let's go and leave these two to handle things here."

The two leaders left, and after making plans to meet with Robin the next morning, Honoria and Asher headed toward Asher's cottage. It would be their last night there before moving into the cottage designated for clan leaders.

However, once they reached his place, neither one of them had the energy to do more than lie down and cuddle before they drifted off to sleep. Even though Honoria's mind was whirling with thoughts, just having Asher's heat and scent surrounding her helped to calm her. Before she knew it, she was fast asleep.

Asher was chained to a chair, blood running down his chest from where his cousin had cut a K into his skin.

A dull pain thudded at the wound. Maybe it would've been more pronounced if Asher hadn't been through so many "persuasion sessions" over the last four years.

And with his dragon unable to do more than loll its head around inside his mind, there wasn't much anger left in him either.

His cousin stood in front of a fire, holding a long piece of metal into it. If not for having various bones broken, skin shredded, or his senses overloaded purposefully for days on end, he might have had a small sense of trepidation.

But he knew what was coming, and nothing short of swearing allegiance to Marcus would stop it.

His cousin would brand him without hesitation.

His cousin pulled the red-hot metal from the fire and looked at him. "All you have to do is pledge yourself to Marcus, and all of this can stop."

It would be easy to give in. A few words from his lips, ones he didn't mean in his heart, and he could finally be reunited with his dragon and see the sky again.

And yet, if he did that, his bastard uncle would win. Asher may be insignificant in the grander scheme of things, but if everyone gave up when it got tough, then no one would be able to eventually help Skyhunter. All of his former students, friends, and family would be forced to live a life of fear, until the day when the clan was no more.

Because in his heart, Asher knew that if Marcus reigned for even five more years in the same way, his uncle would make a move too far. All it'd take was hurting some of the local humans to bring about the end of the clan.

And he didn't want that.

So, yes, giving in would be easier. However, he couldn't do it. While defiance wasn't much, it was all he had.

Trying his best to sit up tall, Asher finally replied, "No. I won't ever serve that narcissistic, power-hungry arsehole for as long as I live."

He swore excitement flashed in his cousin's eyes, but it was gone before he could be sure. His cousin moved to stand in front of him. "Then let's try something new. Maybe it'll be the final push you need to finally break." He lowered his voice. "Because you will *break, Asher. My record is nearly flawless, except for you. So, yes, you'll break."*

And then the bastard pressed the hot metal against his open wound. Asher did his best not to scream, but as his flesh burned, he finally let out a roar. The smell also made his stomach churn, and it took everything he had not to vomit.

His cousin finally removed the metal and Asher slumped in his seat, doing his best to stay awake even though his entire body screamed for him to fall into blissful unconsciousness.

"Did you change your mind?"

He could barely make his lips move, but he murmured, "Never."

The hot metal contacted with his skin again, and all Asher could do was sit there and scream until the blackness consumed him.

Asher sat up, taking a moment to realize he was no longer dreaming and reliving the memory.

His dragon said softly, *I'm here. That bastard can't hurt us anymore.*

Running a hand through his sweat-dampened hair, Asher nearly jumped when a warm hand touched his shoulder.

Honoria's sleepy voice filled the room. "Are you okay, Ash? Did you have a flashback?"

He could brush it off as a bad dream, deflect questions, and try to distract his female another way.

However, Asher had been keeping his past from everyone but the counselor. And while he'd rather Honoria not know about his bloody barbaric imprisonment, not telling her would only keep her at arm's length.

She deserved better.

His dragon chimed in. *Tell her. She deserves more than our dick. She should know all of our weaknesses, too.*

Picking at the sheet with his fingers, he forced himself to answer. "It was one of my nightmares." He paused, and added softly, "As you know, I was tortured during the five years I was imprisoned. Every once in a while, one of the sessions haunts my dreams."

Just hearing Honoria's voice helped to soothe his soul. "If you want to talk, we can. But if you need time, that's okay, too. I love you, Ash, and I just want you to know that I'll always be here if you need me. Don't forget that."

He risked meeting Honoria's eyes, and the love shining there banished his remaining tension from the nightmare. "One day, I will. Maybe not quite yet." He took her hand, brought it to his lips, and kissed the back of it. "But just know it's not because I don't want to tell you. It's just difficult, especially since I came out of it mostly intact, unlike my sister."

Poor Aimee. She'd been so young and determined to follow in his footsteps.

Remembering his teenage sister as she raised her chin in defiance and brushed off any warnings of danger about resisting Marcus, made his throat close up.

His dragon sent threads of comfort to him. *We will find a way to help her.*

Honoria's voice prevented him from replying. "I only know the bare minimum about what happened to your sister. Maybe if you can't talk about your own trials during that time, then how about Aimee's? I can't help her, either, if I don't know what's wrong."

Yes, if he could help his sister even a little, so she could at least talk with others again, then maybe he'd be ready to share his own horrors.

So he briefly told Honoria about how his sister didn't talk with people or her dragon; about how flashing dragon eyes caused her to scream and run away; and about how she wouldn't even set foot outside the cottage, not even to merely see the sky again.

When he finished, Honoria merely stared at him a second. He could tell her brain was whirring. It wasn't long before she spoke again. "I have an idea, if you're willing to hear it?"

Squeezing her hand, he murmured, "Of course."

"Well, how much do you know about Arabella MacLeod?"

"The mate of Lochguard's leader?"

She bobbed her head. "Yes, that's what she is now. However, her past is what I'm talking about."

"I don't know much, beyond the fact something happened with dragon hunters and they set her on fire."

"Right, but she also didn't talk with her dragon for nearly a decade. I don't know all the particulars, but she was afraid to do so, and hid away from everyone but her brother and her clan leader. It took meeting Finn to bring her out completely."

He frowned. "I hope you're not suggesting we look for Aimee's true mate and hope kicking off the mate-claim frenzy brings her back."

"No, no, of course not. Arabella should be attending the gathering with the two other clans next week. What if we ask her to meet with Aimee? I don't know if anything would come of it, but it's at least a shot. Arabella has experiences I could never dream of and might be able to get through to your sister."

Not even Asher, whose dragon had been drugged silent for five years, could fully understand Arabella or Aimee's situation. He'd never been afraid of his beast.

He replied, "I'll have to ask my mother first."

"Or, we could ask Lynne together. After all, Aimee is my family now, too."

His beast spoke up. *Ask her to be our mate, then it will be true in all ways.*

Not right now. Let's get everything settled first.

His dragon muttered something unintelligible and curled into a ball inside his mind.

He focused back on Honoria. "Okay, we'll talk to my mum as soon as we can manage it. Although if she agrees, it may be better for you to ask Arabella than me. The last thing I need is Finn growling at me, thinking I'm doing more than talking with his mate."

She rolled her eyes. "By every account, Finn and Arabella are devoted to each other. Give the male some credit."

It may have only been minutes rather than hours, but Asher's dream was all but forgotten. He rolled carefully, moving his back muscles as little as possible, until Honoria was under him. He moved his face closer to hers. "Right now, there's only one female I want to think of." He kissed her gently, taking her lips in slow caresses. "She's the most clever, beautiful, determined female I know. And I want to claim her whenever I have the chance."

She raised an eyebrow. "So no mention of love?"

"Of course I bloody love you." After a quick, rough kiss, he added, "And if you doubt it at all, I think I need to convince you with both my cock and tongue of how much I love you, Honoria Wakeham."

While claiming her in a proper ceremony before the clan would be ideal, he did the next best thing and let his female know she was his, body and soul. Sure, she had to do most of the heavy lifting because of his injury, but when they both finally fell asleep in each other's arms, he didn't think she minded.

Not to mention no nightmare dared invade his dreams again, not with the female he loved by his side.

CHAPTER TWELVE

The next week flew by in a series of meetings with clan members, interviewing people to fill various positions within what would be Skyhunter's first "enclave of leaders," and filling out the necessary paperwork sent by the Department of Dragon Affairs.

It all happened so fast that Honoria barely had time to find a traditional dragon-shifter dress that would fit her overly tall frame. Yet as she studied her reflection in the mirror, the dark purple dress slung over one shoulder before hugging her waist and flaring out at the hips, cascading to just above the ground, Honoria thought the dress was perfect.

For the first time in a while, a sense of pride surged through her body at the color. Dark purple had been Skyhunter's traditional color for centuries, but every time she'd worn it before, she'd always felt ashamed at what it represented.

But no longer.

Her dragon spoke up. *Of course not. This color now represents us, Asher, and the future.*

Well, the real test will be to see how many others come dressed in the color.

While dragon-shifter traditional dress had been specified, she and Asher had mentioned the color was up to each person's choice.

Just because she saw it as the future didn't mean everyone else would. Marcus had forced many a gathering, even before she'd been shipped off to America, and wearing dark purple had been a requirement. After a while, the color had come to represent everything that had changed—for the worst—inside Skyhunter.

Like many things, it would take time to change the feelings surrounding it.

Asher entered the room, wearing a dark purple, yellow and black plaid outfit. Much like kilts of old, it was slung over one shoulder, wrapped around his waist, and the material encircled his lower half, draping to just below his knees.

The K-shaped scar on his chest was in plain view.

She closed the distance between them and murmured, "Someone's looking sexy tonight."

He snorted. "I'm sure you'd say that even if I wore a skirt made out of ferns."

"Maybe." She placed a hand over his scar. "Are you sure about this, though? I know we talked about you wearing a white shirt."

He shook his head. "Even if it were snowing outside, I'd still go bare-chested. If Arabella MacLeod can walk around not caring about her scars, I can do the same."

She kissed him briefly. "I'm anxious to see if her talking with Aimee tonight will help or not."

"Me, too. But she can't do that until we get the gathering started, which means getting all the leaders to participate in the first dance."

Raising her brows, she tilted her head. "It's not like we can start it yet. Not everyone is here. Besides, we need to greet the other clan leaders in private first." He grunted, and she laughed before adding, "Oh, come on. Bram and Finn's mates are here so there might be a little less bickering."

"So you say," he grumbled.

She kissed him again, more slowly this time, before stepping back and taking his hand. "Let's go. I'll be doing most of the talking anyway. Your job is not to scowl, if you can help it."

Asher scowled.

She lightly hit his side. "Stop it."

He winked. "I'll try. Although I can't make any guarantees."

She motioned toward the door. "Are you done? The sooner we do this, the sooner we can help your sister."

Asher's face turned serious, and he guided her to the door.

~~~

Asher's dragon paced inside his mind as he said, *Why do we have to follow all the formalities? The clan just wants to have a party and finally breathe a sigh of relief.*

This is a party, but including traditions will help it feel more like a dragon-shifter *party.*

His beast grunted. *Someone is bound to stir up trouble.*

Oh, stop it. I know wearing these colors makes you uneasy, but if we can't wear them, how can we expect others to do so?

His beast growled. *They didn't have to wear dirty, torn prison uniforms with the same pattern. Or, at least not the majority of them.*

Even a few weeks ago, wearing the plaid made up of dark purple, black, and yellow would've stirred up a mixture of anger and resentment, not to mention unwanted memories.
~~~

However, the moment he'd seen Honoria in the dark purple traditional dress, he'd started to view the color in another light.

Especially since it made her skin glow and hair gleam brighter.

His beast snorted. *She would look better with nothing on at all.*

There's no bloody way I'm letting the other leaders see her naked.

What if an emergency crops up? She's not going to hide behind a sheet to shift.

They approached the door being used as the waiting area for Stonefire and Lochguard's leaders, and their honored guests. *Shut it. I need to focus.*

Fine. But don't expect me to stay silent the entire evening.

He and Honoria paused in front of the door. Glancing over, he asked, "Ready?"

"Of course. Unlike you, I think this will be fun."

"Later we're going to have to define 'fun' because I think the American clan may have given you the wrong idea."

She rolled her eyes. "Whatever."

The corners of his mouth curved upward. "Maybe you should give classes on how to sound more American. That should be a cinch for you."

Shaking her head, Honoria placed a hand on the doorknob. "As much as I love your teasing, let's save it for later. Skyhunter will be on shaky ground for a while yet. So let's prove we're serious enough to handle all the challenges."

His beast huffed. *If anything, Skyhunter's been too serious.*

That's not what she meant, and you know it.

Asher bobbed his head and they entered the room.

Inside, the Stonefire leader and his mate wore dark red. The Lochguard pair wore a deep, dark blue. Their guests—Protectors he'd learned from the RSVPs—wore the respective colors of their clans.

He grunted his greetings to the leaders before meeting Arabella MacLeod's gaze. Her eyes flicked down to his chest and back again. A smile played on her lips. "Between Snowridge's leader and his three scars on his cheek, me and my burns, and you and your brand, people are going to think some sort of tragedy is a requirement to reach the upper echelons of a dragon-shifter clan."

Everyone went unnaturally still, apart for Arabella. The others never would've brought up the K on his chest. At least, not so soon.

Asher could make a noncommittal noise and change the subject. It would be easy enough.

However, he rather liked that Arabella didn't dance around the issue. And if she could joke about it despite how much more severe the remnants of her torture were, then he should be able to do the same. "You may be on to something. Although I forever hope Honoria's excluded from that requirement."

Finn grinned. "And me as well. We can't have these rugged good looks being tarnished, now, can we?"

Arabella shook her head. "As I always warn you, one day you'll wake up with no hair on your head if you keep bragging about how wonderfully handsome you are."

Finn waggled his brows. "But I am, aren't I, love?"

"I'm not sure I should answer that," Arabella drawled.

Finn leaned down to his mate's ear, murmured something for only her, and Arabella blushed. "Stop it, Finn."

Bram cleared his throat. "May I introduce my mate, Evie Marshall?"

Honoria extended a hand toward the female with dark-red hair and blue eyes standing at Bram's side and said, "Nice to meet you, Evie. I've heard so much about you." Honoria's gaze moved to a tall, blonde-haired female standing beyond Bram. "And you, too, Jane."

It was then that Asher noticed Stonefire's head Protector and his mate, Jane. If he could find some time to talk with the male about the latest security measures on Stonefire, then maybe the night wouldn't be completely boring.

His beast growled. *If we dance with Ria, it won't be boring.*

I know that, dragon. But I'm not big on small talk anymore, and I'm sure we'll have to do plenty of that.

Just be blunt, like Arabella. It will make things more interesting.

Asher battled a smile. *We'll see.*

Honoria had been talking with the females, but finished and looked at Asher. "Should we lead them into the great hall now?"

He offered his arm. "The sooner we get this started, the sooner it'll be over."

Threading her arm through his, she looked over her shoulder. "We have plenty of things to talk about later, so no sneaking off into dark corners. Being enamored with your mates is fine and all, but tonight is too important to risk it. However, if you want some secret locations you can sneak to and ravish each other on the way home, I can share later."

Asher bit the inside of his cheek to keep from smiling. Leave it to Honoria to tell them no hanky-panky now, but she'd gladly give them places to do it outside of Skyhunter. She already fitted into the role of clan leader without really trying.

Of course, he didn't want to test how far she could push the other leaders so soon. So he guided her out of the room and down the corridor leading to the great hall.

It was time to let those invited from Stonefire and Lochguard mingle with his clan members.

Asher only hoped it didn't devolve into some kind of chaos or fight.

Honoria stood next to Asher as Skyhunter's Protectors opened the different doors to the great hall. Members from each of the three clans had waited in different areas as a precaution. As he watched them slowly enter the room, one thing stuck out to him—the Stonefire and Lochguard dragon-shifters quickly mingled with one another. However, apart from a few of the elder Skyhunter members waving at people they had probably known from before Marcus King's time, Honoria and Asher's clan kept to themselves.

Before he could think too much on it, Honoria turned toward him and whispered, "Do you have any ideas of how to get them to talk with one another?"

Staring into her lovely blue eyes, he wished he could instantly erase the worry there. However, they were trying not to show signs of affection in public just yet. So he merely replied, "It's too early to worry. Let's just open the gathering first, and then see if we need to take extra measures."

She nodded, and Asher moved to the front of the dais, where all of the leaders were. Putting his fingers to his lips, he whistled until everyone's attention turned toward the front of the room. Then he said, "Welcome to the first inter-clan gathering on Skyhunter for decades. Stonefire's leader, Bram Moore-Llewellyn, and Lochguard's leader, Finlay Stewart, as well as their mates, are our honored guests for the evening. As you may have noticed, they brought a few of their own clan members along with them, too. And as far as I know, they don't bite."

Finn interrupted, "Aye, well, as long as Skyhunter doesn't bite first. After that, it becomes fair game and us Scots are pretty skilled with our teeth."

He winked, and chuckles rolled across the room.

Asher didn't have that particular skill set—and wasn't sure he ever would—but he suspected Honoria would be the teasing relief in the long run.

Focusing back on the crowd, Asher continued. "I know we were taught to avoid other dragon clans like the plague under the former leader. However, Stonefire and Lochguard are our allies now. And to show they won't bite, Honoria and I will be the first examples."

Even though Asher hadn't cleared it with the other clan leaders, he was fairly sure they'd be okay with his idea if it meant strengthening ties between the clans.

His beast grunted. *Let's hope so. I'd rather not duel tonight.*

Ignoring his dragon, Asher turned toward Arabella and put out a hand, palm up. Making sure his voice projected so everyone could hear, he asked, "May I have the first dance?"

The dragonwoman didn't even blink and placed her hand in his. "Of course." Finn growled, and she whispered low enough the crowd below shouldn't be able to hear her, even with their super-sensitive dragon-shifter hearing, "There's no need to be jealous. We discussed Honoria and Asher earlier. Besides, it's not as if he's going to whisk me away, along with three extremely lively triplets, to some cave where he'd merely endure an endless line of nappy changes, cries, and feedings."

Asher blinked, but thankfully, Finn spoke so he didn't have to. "Aye, fine." He pierced Asher with a serious look.

"But keep your hands from wandering, aye?"

Bram's mate sighed and went over to Finn. "I didn't think it was possible, but you're worse than Bram. Come on, Finn, you can dance with me. I'm not about to force Honoria to do it with you so soon."

Finn muttered, "What does that mean?"

Bram walked over to Honoria. "Consider yourself lucky. Finn's charm is best taken in small doses."

Some people might be overwhelmed with how the other leaders and their mates acted, but now that the trials were over and his future was somewhat more certain, he enjoyed it more than before. Maybe someday he could be more easygoing with the other leaders.

Especially if he had Honoria at his side, as his mate.

His beast spoke up. *Of course we'll have her. And Honoria calms us down, so we won't be so wary around the other leaders. Although I hope we don't get quite as close to the other males as Finn and Bram are with each other. The Scottish dragonman is exhausting.*

He snorted. *We agree on that.*

Arabella's voice prevented his beast from replying. "Care to share what your dragon said?"

"Probably not."

"If it's about Finn, don't worry about offending me and feel free to tell me. He can be a bit much at first, but he's a very dedicated leader and would do anything for his family and clan." She lowered her voice. "The best way to deal with him is to be straightforward and try to ignore the charm. It can be hard sometimes—even I can't resist his smiles every once in a while—but if you do, then you'll get to know him better. After all, everyone has different types of armor to hide behind."

The dragonwoman was wise for her years, that much was obvious.

Unsure of what to say to that, especially since Asher hadn't been forced into a lot of social situations with new people for years, he merely nodded and motioned toward the main floor. "How about we move into position for the dance?"

Arabella didn't try to take control as he led her down the stairs of the dais and to the center of the floor, where the dancing would take place.

Once all three couples were ready, the music came on and they began dancing.

Asher had been practicing with Honoria for the last few days—sometimes naked, to really test his concentration skills—so he at least didn't step on Arabella's feet as they moved about the room.

Still, he didn't know exactly what to say to her. Honoria had handled talking with the dragonwoman about meeting with his sister.

His beast spoke up. *Then just ask her about it. She's a dragon-shifter, not a human and won't be offended.*

So you want people to just bring up our torture whenever they feel like it?

We're not asking about her pain, just what she plans to do with Aimee.

Arabella's voice cut through his thoughts. "You remind me a little of my brother."

He frowned. "Pardon?"

"My brother, Tristan. He's not overly talkative, either. And he has the same sense of quiet power."

"Um, thank you?"

Arabella laughed, and Asher caught a glare from Finn. However, he paid it no heed and decided changing the subject would be easier. Otherwise, Finn may cut in and Asher would never have a chance to ask for information.

After making an easy turn, he said, "Ria said you'd be meeting with my sister tomorrow morning. Thank you."

She raised a dark eyebrow. "For what? I haven't done anything yet."

"Just coming is a big deal, and you know it. Finn may be leader, but he wouldn't take a fool for a mate."

"No, I'm not a fool. And good you recognize it." She paused, and Asher wondered if he'd gone too far. But then her face softened as she added, "I know what it's like to be afraid of your inner dragon, and just know that you asking for help shows how much you care for your sister."

He should say thanks and move the conversation to something lighter. But it was his sister they were talking about, and so he pushed. "Will you be able to help her at all?"

"I don't know. However, that doesn't mean I won't try."

His slight optimism faded a fraction. As if sensing his change in mood, Arabella added, "Although there is one thing I wanted to ask you before I met with Aimee." He arched his brows in question, and she asked, "Would you be willing to have her come to Lochguard, if she agrees?" He opened his mouth to say absolutely not—they may be allies, but they were new allies, and there was a lot he didn't know about the other clans—but she beat him to it. "And before you deny me outright, just listen for a minute, okay? Being on Skyhunter reminds her of everything that happened. Ria said your sister never left the cottage, either. I suspect it's because of the memories. It was a little different for me—I wasn't tortured inside the clan. However, I couldn't stand the looks of pity from everyone and closed myself off, thinking it would be easier. Only fostering with another clan and being accepted by Finn's family eventually made me come out of my shell. It could be the case that Aimee needs to leave Skyhunter and be somewhere new, somewhere not filled with terror, pain, and loss so she can heal. Lochguard would be a nice escape, and my in-laws will greet her with open arms whenever she's ready. Will you at least consider allowing Aimee to come to Lochguard?"

While he'd thought Honoria's suggestion of the dragonwoman had been an interesting idea, hearing more of the specifics of her situation only convinced him more that Arabella MacLeod might indeed be the one to help his sister.

Even if it meant losing her in the short term.

His dragon spoke up. *Mum won't like it.*

Then maybe she should go with her.

He replied to Arabella, "I can't make the decision for Aimee or my mother. However, if Aimee somehow conveys she wants that, then I will think about it."

"And what if I can't break through to her whilst on Skyhunter?"

"Then ask my mother if the pair of them could go with you. If my mum says yes, then most likely I'll let them go. Even though I want to trust you easily, I'll need to hash out the finer details with Finn concerning Aimee's safety."

Arabella nodded. "I know merely thinking about sending your sister away is hard for you, and it shows the seeds of trust you're planting. If it helps you at all, then I vow on all three of my children's lives that if Aimee comes to Lochguard, I will watch over her like my own sister."

Dragon-shifters treasured children, so Arabella making such a vow spoke volumes about how serious she would take her duties, if they materialized.

His beast spoke up. *I think she's being genuine and wants to help Aimee. So far, I like her best of the other clan members.*

Asher bowed his head a second. "Thank you, I acknowledge your vow." The final notes of the song drifted in the air. "Although shouldn't you discuss it with your mate first?"

Arabella shrugged one shoulder. "In this sort of situation, he'll have my back. Finn's a big softie inside and has had to deal with a few females needing to heal in their own way. He'll look out for your sister as much as me. No, wait, probably even more. He's quite overprotective in his brotherly role, maybe even more so than when he goes all growly and protective mate-like."

The song ended, and exactly two seconds later, Finn was at Arabella's side. He kept his voice low, for their ears only. "You two seemed rather cozy during the dance."

Arabella leaned against her mate and patted his chest. "It was something important, about his sister."

Finn's irritation vanished. "Oh, aye?"

"I'll tell you when we're alone." Arabella smiled at Asher. "Thanks for the dance. If, for some reason, I don't get to speak with you again tonight, I'll stop by your mother's house tomorrow morning and we can chat after."

Asher nodded, and the pair walked away, toward a ginger-haired male Asher recognized—Fraser MacKenzie.

He'd since learned the irritating male had not only helped save his life but was also Finn's cousin. Which meant he would be subjecting Aimee to the bastard if he let her go to Lochguard.

His beast huffed. *He's happily mated, and you have to admit, our sister needs a little levity.*

Honoria touched his bicep, garnering his attention. Once he met her gaze, she said, "You two seemed to be talking about something serious. Should I be worried?"

What he wouldn't give to pull Honoria close and kiss the living shit out of her, in front of everyone, so they would know she was his.

Instead, he replied, "Yes, we discussed Aimee. We can

talk more later." He motioned toward the mostly segregated Skyhunter bunch on one side, and the Lochguard and Stonefire crowd on the other. "Did you have an idea of how to bring them together?"

"Actually, Bram mentioned something when we were dancing. Apparently, there's an old English dragon-shifter tradition for when several clans get together. It has to do with the first proper dance after the leaders have theirs. Everyone is supposed to dance with a dragon not from their home, or be forced to leave the great hall."

"Um, Ria, most of Skyhunter probably would *want* to leave."

She put up a hand. "Let me finish. They leave, but then they have to jump in the nearest lake or river before being let back onto the clan's lands."

"I still don't think it'll work. We're trying to get people to stay on Skyhunter, not leave it."

"Oh, come on, Ash. We could change it to those who don't dance will be gathered together and sprayed with a garden hose by a family member. It'll be fun, but also a sort of punishment. After all, England isn't exactly a tropical island and warm all year round."

"How is being wet and cold supposed to be fun, exactly?" he drawled.

She sighed. "Just let me try, okay? We have to do something."

Her hand brushed against his, and a sizzle traveled up his arm. His beast laughed. *Are you really going to be able to deny her? Just think, if you give in, she'll probably reward us later.*

Making her happy should be enough.

Right, tell yourself that. Meanwhile, I'll be thinking of the best way to claim her as ours and make her scream.

Not wanting to encourage his beast and risk a hard cock,

especially given the kilt-like attire with nothing to hide it, he replied, “Okay, try it. But you’re going to be in charge of it all.”

Her eyes lit up and she clapped. “Yay, this should be fun. And even though I’ll be in charge, you should come up onto the dais with me, for support. A united front, and all that.”

His dragon said, *I know a way we can be united.*

I want Ria naked and under us as much as you do, but can you tame it down for an hour or two?

Maybe we should go for a dunk in an icy, cold lake.

That’s unhelpful.

His beast huffed. *Fine. I’ll try to hold back, but I can’t make any promises.*

Honoria moved toward the dais, and he followed. The night was already interesting. Maybe by the end of it, everyone on Skyhunter would be a little different from the day before, in a good way.

CHAPTER THIRTEEN

As the weak sunlight filtered into their kitchen the following morning, Honoria kept glancing at Asher. He wasn't a chatty male by nature, but he was even quieter than before.

Not that she could blame him. While the gathering had been mostly a success—almost everyone had participated in at least the first dance, and only one fight had erupted between two drunk dragonmen from different clans—her male's mind was on something else.

Since they were alone in their cottage, Honoria didn't hesitate to stand, move, and settle herself into Asher's lap. His arms instantly went around her, and she murmured, "I know you want to be there with your sister, but Arabella thinks meeting with Aimee one-on-one is her best chance at getting through to her."

He sighed as he rubbed circles on her lower back. "I know. But if this doesn't work, I'm not sure what else we can do."

Caressing his cheek, she answered, "We'll keep searching until we find something to help her, I promise."

He tightened his hold on her. "You're amazing, Honoria Wakeham. Have I told you I love you today yet?"

The corner of her mouth kicked up. "Only twice. And you know how I like to hear it at least five times."

"I love you." He moved his head a fraction closer. "I love you." And again. "I love you."

She closed the distance between them and kissed him. Asher slid his tongue inside her mouth and stroked every inch of it, his actions more demanding than normal.

Her dragon spoke up. *He needs us. I'll even let him take control this time, if it'll make him worry less.*

As much as Honoria wanted Asher anytime she could get him alone, she didn't think now was the right time; Asher's mother could call at any second with an update.

So she merely continued kissing her male until Asher's mobile phone rang. Since the ringtone was the one used specifically for his mother, Honoria broke the kiss.

He picked up the phone and said, "Yes?"

Because she was sitting in his lap, it was easy to hear his mother's reply. "Aimee wants to go to Lochguard."

She sat up taller at that comment.

Asher asked, "Did she finally talk?"

"Not exactly. Arabella had some cards with her, with various choices on them. When asked if she wanted to go to Lochguard for a while and stay with her, Aimee quickly grabbed the card that said 'Yes, I want to go to Lochguard,' and held it out to Ara. Just to make sure, Arabella shuffled the cards on the table, repeated the question, and Aimee picked the same card." His mother paused and asked, "Will you let us go?"

She watched Asher's face closely. At the brief flash of hope, her heart melted.

He said, "If that's what you both want, then yes."

"It is. After all, this is the most responsive your sister has been since, since..."

His mother's voice cracked, and Asher murmured, "I know, Mum. And we'll give her a chance. I'll be over right away."

"Please do. Arabella needs to leave soon, but wants to ensure you agree first. I'd rather not keep her waiting. After all, she just wants to get back to her own children."

"Thanks, Mum. See you soon."

Asher clicked off the phone and stared at it. "Aimee..."

Honoria took his cheeks between her hands and gently forced him to meet her gaze. "I'm sure she'll be talking again before you know it. One day, you'll have your little sister back, just wait and see."

Placing a hand over hers, he nodded. "I sure hope so."

Asher didn't allow many to see his weaknesses, but with her, he didn't try to hide his mixture of worry and apprehension.

What Honoria wouldn't do to make him and his sister simply be happy again. Even if she couldn't make the siblings forget all of the awful things that had been done to them, a day free of memories or flashbacks would be a good first step.

Her beast spoke up. *If he didn't remember those things, then he wouldn't be who he is now. We can't change the past, but we can make a bloody good future together. Maybe you can try harder to accomplish that.*

Not wanting to discuss mates or the fact Asher wasn't yet theirs officially with her dragon, Honoria kissed Asher quickly. Then she slid off his lap and motioned toward the door. "Come on. If we can confirm details with Arabella and Finn this morning, then maybe Aimee can be driven to Lochguard either today or tomorrow. That way she can start healing as soon as possible."

As they walked out of the cottage, Asher said, "I'll miss her, but it's her best shot. She had such fire as a teenager.

All I can do is hope you get to see that side of her, even if it's not quite as strong as before."

She lightly brushed his arm. "We'll just have to trust Arabella."

He nodded. "It's strange trusting someone so soon, but there's something about the dragonwoman that makes me believe her."

"I think it's the specific circumstance. She's gone through something similar and came out of it on the other side."

"Right." He met her gaze. "Thanks for suggesting it originally, Ria. I'm not sure I would've thought of it."

She lightly touched his hand again. "There's no need for thanks. We're a team, meaning we should help the other when needed. And yes, it means for more than just clan issues. I hope you remember that."

He nodded. "I do."

Asher fell silent, thinking about who knew what. There were times to push and ask what he thought, but considering his sister was going to be leaving them for an untold amount of time, she figured he needed a little peace to come to grips with it.

So they walked the rest of the way in a comfortable silence. Well, as comfortable as they could be given Asher would soon be saying goodbye to his mum and sister.

True, Honoria hadn't even had the chance to say goodbye to her parents in the end, but that was different. Aimee and Lynne King weren't going to be imprisoned and executed. The farewell this morning would be sad, but also happy because it gave them hope.

And if there was something Skyhunter could do with, it was more hope.

Later that evening, Asher stood across from his mother and sister, Honoria waiting outside if he needed her, and he tried to think of what to say to his family.

It didn't help that Aimee had been given a sedative to ensure she made the twelve-hour car ride from Skyhunter up to Lochguard in the Scottish Highlands. To be honest, she might be too far out of it to even remember what he said to her.

And yet, he didn't want to send her off without some words of brotherly love.

Of course, while it was easy to say affectionate words with Honoria, he didn't do it often with others.

His beast growled, and Asher closed his eyes a second so Aimee couldn't see his pupils change to slits. *It's not that hard. It's the truth—we love them. Stop hesitating. When you do, it doesn't reflect strength, which we need to do as often as we can right now.*

We're standing inside Mum's cottage. I doubt anyone has hidden cameras in here. Now, hush. We can't risk upsetting Aimee, or it'll delay her departure even more.

Fine. I'll be quiet until she leaves.

His beast walked in a circle before settling down, wrapping his tail around his body, and laying his head on top of it.

Asher opened his eyes and focused on his mother first. "Let me know if you need anything. And if they so much as look at you funny, tell me and I'll sort it out."

His mother smiled. "I've handled far worse, Asher. I'll be fine."

She engulfed him in a hug, and he murmured, "I love you, Mum. It'll be strange with you gone. But if it means helping Aimee, I'd do far more than say goodbye to accomplish it."

After squeezing him tightly, his mother released him. "I didn't survive Marcus's reign merely so I could flee afterward. We'll be back, and not just because my handsome son is one-half of the leadership, either. I know you'll do a brilliant job, Asher." She lowered her voice. "Maybe I'll come back for a special occasion?"

He was grateful that Honoria had given him a few minutes alone with his mother and sister. Otherwise, his mum might be extracting promises of a mating before they even knew it. Lynne King could be devious if she wanted, albeit was always with love. "If it happens, I'll let you know."

His mother raised her brows. "If? More like, when. I predicted that when you two were children. I have a sense for these things."

He gave a noncommittal grunt, hoping that would be the end of it. Arguing with his mother right before she left for who knew how long wasn't the sendoff he wanted to give her.

His mum motioned toward Aimee. "I'll give you a minute alone with your sister. Let me know when you're done, and I'll collect her."

Once his mother left, he turned toward Aimee.

He didn't like the way her eyes were half closed or the fact she looked about ready to slump to one side in the chair.

But he knew the drugs were necessary, otherwise she'd never make the journey.

And she needed to make the journey. More than ever, he was convinced of how she needed to leave Skyhunter to forget about the horrors of her imprisonment.

His inner dragon didn't speak, but sent him waves of encouragement. They always helped, and one day, Aimee would have the same again.

He refused to believe otherwise.

Squatting down to her eye level, he said, "Don't let the Scottish dragons push you too far. If it's too much, you say so. And remember, I'm always a phone call away."

Aimee said nothing. She didn't even move her head.

He hated her like this, absolutely hated it.

But he kept a smile on his face and hid his true feelings. "I'll miss you, Aims. I'm not sure I'll be able to visit you anytime soon, but I'll always be thinking of you."

There was no response from his sister.

He wanted to kiss her cheek or give her a hug, but couldn't risk an episode. So he merely said, "I'll fetch Mum, and you can be off to start your new life."

Once he did, his mother managed to get Aimee into a car.

Honoria moved to his side and together, they watched them drive away.

As his mother and sister vanished from sight, Honoria took his hand. In that instant, something became crystal clear to him. His sister and mother may never return to Skyhunter. Honoria was his everything now, and he needed to make it official.

He tugged her back into his mother's house and pulled her up against his chest. Cupping her cheek, he murmured, "I have something to ask you."

She tilted her head a fraction. "What is it?"

Asher knew what he wanted and didn't hesitate. "Will you be my mate?"

She blinked. "Huh?"

"Honoria Wakeham, will you do me the honor of becoming my mate?"

"I want to scream yes, but why the change in attitude? I believe you said something about waiting until the clan is more stable."

"Together, I know we'll make it stable. But I can't risk losing you, Ria. And I want the world to know you're mine."

"More like you're mine."

The corner of his mouth ticked up. "I think it can be both."

She smiled, and the world instantly became brighter. "I think so, too. And yes, I'll be your mate, Asher King. And not just because I want to do this anytime I want and stop sneaking around."

Pulling his head down, Honoria kissed him.

As he put every bit of love he had into that kiss, both man and beast couldn't wait for the mating ceremony. It would be Skyhunter's first since they'd taken over, and in a way, it was the most fitting.

Two former lovers torn apart by hate had found their way back home, into the arms of each other. Skyhunter would start over with love.

And over the next few hours, Asher showed Honoria how much he loved her privately, over and over again, until they both drifted off to sleep, wrapped around each other, as if proving to the world they'd never let each other go.

EPILOGUE

Years Later

Honoria had never been more grateful that her newborn son liked to sleep. A lot. A gale-force wind could blow through the area, and he wouldn't bat an eyelash.

While introducing new babies to the clan was important, it wasn't exactly quiet inside the great hall. Under the circumstances, a sleeping baby was rare indeed.

Her beast grunted. *It's all thanks to Aimee's in-laws. The Scots are incorrigible.*

Skyhunter has its fair share of rambunctious younger folk, too.

Nowhere near as bad as them. I wouldn't put it past them to fire up some bagpipes at some point. The grandfather, especially, will *cause trouble before the night is done.*

Archie is harmless.

Only because it's a special night will I pretend you don't know his reputation.

Archie MacAllister had spent a lifetime battling with his neighbor over a property border dispute. Apparently, dropping boulders from the sky in dragon form wasn't unheard of between the pair.

She glanced over at Aimee and her mate, a Scottish dragon-shifter from Lochguard, and couldn't help but smile at the large amount of family standing around her. The MacAllisters were almost all outgoing to begin with, so add in some mates and small children, and Honoria doubted there was ever truly peace and quiet when they all got together.

Honoria said to her dragon, *It could be a lot worse than a few boisterous Scots. Or have you forgotten how difficult the first year was, trying to convince everyone that Asher and I wouldn't turn into dictators like Marcus?*

Her beast huffed. *I'm sure their dragons trusted us a lot sooner. I don't understand their human halves at all. We did one improvement and good after another—including fosters and inter-clan Protector drills. And still, many resisted.*

It doesn't matter how long it took, all that matters is how it convinced them in the end.

Asher finally made his way up the dais, cutting her conversation short with her beast. He kissed their son Julian's forehead, and then Honoria's lips. He whispered, "Sorry, love. It seems everyone has advice to offer." He lowered his voice for her ears only. "And while my dragon thought telling them to sod off would be the best remedy, I somehow resisted."

She raised an eyebrow. "If you think your restraint merits praise, then you'll be waiting a long time. I think every former or current mother on Skyhunter has stopped by to tell me how to raise Julian. Not once, or even twice. I reckon at least five times apiece."

Asher's lips twitched. "It just means they care."

"Right, while the males will merely smack you on the

back and say good job. Somehow, that doesn't seem fair."

"We divide everything, remember? This is just one of those circumstances when it falls to you."

She stuck out a tongue a second before adding, "Then you can take on the charming role for the evening. After all those one-on-ones with the females, I'm too tired to do it."

"I somehow don't believe you're too tired to be yourself."

"What, that I'm tired to the bone and that may have affected my personality a little? Of course it's the truth."

"Tired from the baby, yes, that's a given. But you *like* talking to others. Me, not so much."

"What about all the training and flying sessions you do with the students?"

Asher's back had healed properly and ever since, he'd been teaching as much as his schedule allowed.

Her mate grunted. "That's different. They want to learn something, and I have the knowledge. It's a bloody big difference from trying to feign interest in someone's vegetable garden."

She bit her lip to keep from laughing. One of the clan members was quite enthusiastic about his plants, to the point that if a dragon hunter attack happened, he'd run to guard them from being destroyed.

Pushing her amusement aside, she shrugged and then rearranged the blanket around Julian. "Equal shares, remember? I put up with the mothers, so it's your turn."

He sighed. "Fine. But only because I love you."

She beamed. "It's amazing how often that works in my favor." He shook his head, but she leaned over and kissed him quickly. "I love you, too, Asher King. Now, let's welcome our son to the clan properly."

Asher moved to the front of the dais, and Honoria stood beside him. As he quieted down the clan, it was a stark contrast to their very first clan meeting. Back then, people had fallen silent right away. However, this time it took Asher nearly three minutes to get the crowd mostly silent.

And yet, she couldn't help but smile at all. It'd taken years, but Skyhunter was mostly healed and a cohesive unit more times than not. Add in the presence of the MacAllisters from Lochguard, and how many from Skyhunter greeted one or more of them as friends, and it was an even greater contrast to the early days.

Staring down at her sleeping son's face, happiness flooded her body. The clan was doing well, she loved Asher more than ever before, and their family had welcomed their beautiful boy two weeks ago.

Add in the solid alliances with the other dragon clans and budding relationships with the neighboring humans, and it was hard to believe Honoria's parents had sent her away from Skyhunter in the dead of night almost twenty years ago.

Asher finally had the crowd quiet, and he projected his voice so that even the few humans in attendance could hear him. "That may be a new record in getting your attention. Maybe next time we can work on that?"

The old Scottish dragonman Archie shouted, "I always have my bagpipes, laddie. Just say the word, and I'll get everyone quiet, aye?"

To his credit, Asher didn't frown. "Thank you, but I'd rather not wake my son. Speaking of which, that's why we're all gathered here today, to celebrate Julian King's arrival to the clan. And while we'll do the tattoo design presentation a little later, Skyhunter, please say hello to our newest addition and let him know how much we welcome him."

Asher gently took Julian with one hand under his head and the other under his bum. He lifted their baby carefully over his head. "Say hello to Julian, one and all."

Honoria held her breath as everyone cheered, but her son didn't so much as stir.

Her beast spoke up. *Stop worrying so much. It's nice he only cries when hungry or when he needs a nappy change. It could be much worse, like that one mother.*

There was a female on Skyhunter who had a pair of twins that cried whenever they left home. *The doctor said they were healthy, and I'm sure they'll grow out of it.*

Asher brought Julian back down and cuddled him against his chest. "Now, have fun and enjoy the celebration. Ria and I will be down shortly so that everyone can perform their official welcome greetings to the baby."

They both noticed Archie stand up on a chair. How the male could do it so nimbly—he had to be in his seventies—she had no idea.

Asher spoke before Archie could. "And no singing or bagpipes until the young ones are put down for the night. We'll leave that to the adult part of the celebration."

The old male sighed, and his grandchildren helped him off the chair. Honoria met Aimee's eyes, and they shared a smile.

But then Archie was off doing something else, and Aimee went to help her mate and his siblings.

Honoria took the brief minute of quiet to lean against her mate and trace her son's cheek. "I love you, Julian." She glanced up at Asher. "And I love you, too, Ash."

"Not as much as I love you, Ria."

Before she could argue the point—they seemed to do that often—he leaned down and kissed her. As he took his time caressing the inside of her mouth and letting her know with each stroke how much he cared for her, she forgot about everything but him, her, and the little bundle under her fingers.

Years ago, when she'd won the right to be a co-leader of Skyhunter, she'd gained more than a clan to take care of. She'd found the love of her life.

And she couldn't wait to see what else the future held for them.

AUTHOR'S NOTE

Over the years, I've received a lot of messages and emails asking about other dragon clans around the world. There's just so much going on in the Stonefire and Lochguard series that I didn't know if I'd ever get to them. Then it hit me—start a loosely related spinoffs series where each book would be about a different clan. And so, the Stonefire Dragons Universe series was born.

Skyhunter was a clan without a leader and was the perfect starting place. The second book will be about the Welsh dragon clan and its leader, Rhydian. (*Transforming Snowridge*) After that, we'll start exploring clans outside of the UK and Ireland. Since these books are more standalone-ish, it opens a lot of doors. Stonefire and Lochguard will always be in the background of this series since they're at the forefront of change. However, situations vary around the world. Some things are similar, but there are differences, too. I can't wait to share it all with my readers. Not to mention this series gives me mini-breaks from my two main dragon series while still giving you a dragon fix.

Getting this book out requires a lot of help from others and I'm grateful to the following people:

—To my editor, Becky Johnson, and her team at Hot Tree Editing. They forever hold me to high standards and push me to do better.

—To my cover artist, Clarissa Yeo of Yocla Designs. She is amazing at showing me covers I didn't even know I wanted. *Winning Skyhunter* is definitely one of my favorites to date.

—To my team of beta readers: Sabrina D., Donna H., Sandy H. and Iliana G. These women all seem to catch different typos and help make my books as error-free as possible.

And lastly, thanks to you, the reader. I had to push back the release date of some of my books to take a break, and this was a nice way to come back to my dragons. All of your support, comments, and enthusiasm help keep my dragon-shifter universe going.

The next dragon book will be *The Dragon's Discovery*, about Alistair Boyd. A lot of readers have clamored for his story, and the wait is nearly over! Turn the page for some sneak peeks and I hope to see you at the end of the next book.

Coming Early Summer 2019

The Dragon's Discovery
(Lochguard Highland Dragons #6)

The Department of Dragon Affairs sends Dr. Kiyana Barnes to Lochguard with a group of human women open to having dragon mates. She's supposed to help them adjust to being around dragon-shifters while also observing how the clan works on a day-to-day basis. She most definitely isn't supposed to notice how one look from a certain dragonman teacher sets her skin on fire, let alone ask him to kiss her in a weak moment, given her past.

Alistair Boyd spends most of his time in the clan's archives, searching for a solution to fulfill the vow he made to himself three years ago. However, when his clan leader orders him to educate the latest group of humans to come to Lochguard, he has no choice but to cut back and do his clan duty. One of the females in particular catches his eye, but he tries to resist her. After all, he made an important vow. One that includes staying away from females until it's complete.

One weak moment results in a kiss that changes both Kiyana and Alistair's lives forever. Unfortunately, a clan emergency means keeping Alistair's dragon silent, for more days than he'd like. Will Alistair's duty to clan end up harming his dragon and pushing away the woman who is his second chance? Or, will he beat the clock to have everything he didn't know he wanted?

Do you enjoy laugh-out-loud romantic comedies?

Crazy Scottish Love
(Love in Scotland #1)

Tired of the online dating scene and her nagging mother, Donella Spencer braves her eccentric extended family and heads for a month-long visit to Scotland to stay with them. As long as she keeps to herself and avoids her family as much as possible, it should be easy to relax, right?

What she doesn't count on is running into Robbie Campbell, the guy who tried so hard to ditch her nearly twenty years ago that it took a search and rescue team to save her. Not only that, she doesn't expect to fall for Robbie's daughter's big, brown eyes and agree to hold a themed costume party for Donella's 31st birthday. One that involves her relatives dressing in nineteenth century safari garb and dusty, old animal outfits.

And none of that even begins to address her grandmother's attempts to matchmake and marry off Donella within the month.

It's going to be one long, trying summer in Scotland. However, sometimes the strangest situations can show what someone needs in life. Because if Donella falls in love with a man who can put up with her family, her happy ending may finally be in sight.

Provided her relatives don't drive her crazy first.

——————

Crazy Scottish Love is now available in paperback.

About the Author

Jessie Donovan has sold over half a million books, has given away hundreds of thousands more to readers for free, and has even hit the *NY Times* and *USA Today* bestseller lists. She is best known for her dragon-shifter series, but also writes about magic users, aliens, and even has a crazy romantic comedy series set in Scotland. When not reading a book, attempting to tame her yard, or traipsing around some foreign country on a shoestring, she can often be found interacting with her readers on Facebook. She lives near Seattle, where, yes, it rains a lot but it also makes everything green.

Visit her website at: www.JessieDonovan.com

Printed in Great Britain
by Amazon